His heated gaze never veered from her eyes...

"This isn't smart," Tandy murmured.

Wyatt continued to smile softly and pulled her onto his lap, where he kissed her again. A kiss that went deeper and lasted longer.

It lasted so long her fingers curled into the fabric of his shirt. Once they broke apart, Tandy loosened a hand and ran a tentative finger over his lips. "This could easily lead to more. But we have to be realistic."

"How so?"

"I have obligations. Namely a son and a ranch."

"Neither of which I'd do anything to hurt."

She sighed. "You're a good man. I know you'd never mean to hurt me or Scotty. But we both know your job is going to take you away. I can't do a one-night stand. Or even one week or one month."

Closing his eyes, Wyatt set his forehead against hers.

"I can promise you tonight."

Dear Reader,

Although this story is all fiction, I first became interested in the return to the wilds of the Mexican gray wolf shortly after we moved to Tucson. We visited and became members of the Arizona-Sonora Desert Museum, which presents desert wild animals in their natural habitats. At our first visit, the arena for the Mexican gray wolf was empty. A docent explained they were about to get their first pair of the beautiful but almost extinct wolves. And even though there was resistance from area ranchers, a program to repatriate the Mexican gray was taking shape.

That was quite a while ago. The program is ongoing and rancher resentment remains. However, those who work in the Western states wildlife program are always trying new ideas to help wolves and ranchers coexist peacefully. I gave Wyatt Hunt and Tandy Graham jobs of loving ranch life, each other and wolves. I hope you enjoy reading about their struggles.

Readers can contact me via mail at 7739 E. Broadway Blvd #101 Tucson, AZ 85710-3941, or email me at rdfox@cox.net, or via my website, korynna.com/rozfox.

Sincerely,

Roz Denny Fox

MARRYING THE RANCHER

—

Roz Denny Fox

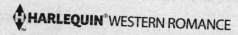
HARLEQUIN® WESTERN ROMANCE

Recycling programs
for this product may
not exist in your area.

ISBN-13: 978-0-373-75779-4

Marrying the Rancher

www.Harlequin.com

Printed in U.S.A.

Roz Denny Fox's first book was published by Harlequin in 1990. She writes for several Harlequin lines and her books are published worldwide in a number of languages. Roz's warm home-and-family-focused love stories have been nominated for various industry awards, including the Romance Writers of America's RITA® Award, the Holt Medallion, the Golden Quill and others. Roz has been a member of the Romance Writers of America since 1987 and is currently a member of Tucson's Saguaro Romance Writers, where she has received the Barbara Award for outstanding chapter service. In 2013 Roz received her fifty-book pin from Harlequin. Readers can contact her on Facebook, at rdfox@cox.net, or visit her website at korynna.com/rozfox.

Books by Roz Denny Fox

Harlequin Western Romance

Snowy Owl Ranchers

His Ranch or Hers
A Maverick's Heart
A Montana Christmas Reunion

Harlequin American Romance

The Maverick Returns
Duke: Deputy Cowboy
Texas Dad
Texas Mom

Visit the Author Profile page
at Harlequin.com for more titles.

This book is dedicated to the many people who work at and volunteer with the Arizona-Sonora Desert Museum. It sits amid cacti and boulders on ninety-eight natural acres. If you have the opportunity to come to Tucson I hope you'll schedule a visit to the museum.

Chapter One

"Ms. Graham, you're the reason the Aravaipa Cattle and Sheep Ranchers Association called this emergency meeting." Preston Hicks sauntered down the grange hall aisle and loomed over where Tandy sat with an arm around her son, Scotty. He'd fallen asleep but came sharply awake at the man's loud verbal attack.

Tandy and Scotty had arrived late and slipped into empty seats in the back row. Stymied as to why she was being singled out, she glanced surreptitiously around, but saw only stern ranchers she probably once knew but hadn't seen in a dozen years.

"What's your problem? I've only operated Spiritridge Ranch a couple of months. I haven't fully rebuilt a herd." Recognizing her sleepy son probably shouldn't be here, she gathered him closer. He wouldn't have come except that as a newly single mom, she'd had no one to leave him with. And the message left on her answering machine had indicated this meeting was important.

Hicks, her closest neighbor and the president of the association, glared down at her from his lofty height and hooked his thumbs over a belt circling his portly belly. "I offered to buy your father's ranch. Since it's doubtful you know a thing about raising cattle, all of us expect sooner or later you'll fail. It would've been smarter if you'd stayed in the army and let me have the ranch."

Garnering murmurs of agreement in the room, the man hitched his pants higher.

"I beg your pardon! I grew up here," Tandy asserted.

"Yeah, well, I don't recall you helped your pa work cattle."

"Because I was busy with schoolwork and sports."

He wagged a beefy finger in her face. "The past is over. What everyone here agrees with is that you can't rent a casita to that damned wolf man. We know Curt, rest his soul, had the poor judgment to let Game and Fish come into our Eastern Arizona sector to do their dirty work after old-timers had rid the area of predators. No one wanted to hound Curt, him being so sick and all. You're a different story. You're a Johnny-come-lately who has no business messing in here at all."

"You mean a Janie-come-lately," called an equally paunchy man, slapping a worn ten-gallon hat on his knee. His comment caused the room full of men to erupt in snickers while Tandy pondered how little time she'd had as a kid to help her dad with the ranch. But she'd loved it. After all, it had been her home.

"We don't want that government fella here," shouted someone Tandy couldn't see. That sufficed to jar her out of her memories. "And we don't need you enabling him, missy. You understand?"

"Mama!" Scotty tugged on his mother's sleeve. "I'm scared. Why are those men yelling at you? I wish we hadn't moved here."

"Shh. Don't be scared." She brushed the boy's sandy-colored hair with a reassuring hand before turning her attention to her first accoster. "Mr. Hunt hasn't shown up yet. How do you know he inquired if his old rental was available?"

"Not that I have to tell you, but Hunt arranged to have his mail delivered out to Spiritridge along with yours starting tomorrow. Roy Wilkerson's wife works at the post office. She took his call and passed on the bad news. You need to send him packing."

"I believe that's my decision." Tandy stood up, squeezing herself and Scotty past the man blocking the aisle with his bulk. She paused briefly to dismiss him with a scowl, along with the others in the room who'd turned in their chairs to stare, apparently all in solidarity with their spokesman.

Lifting her chin, she said loudly, "When my dad was sick and dying of prostate cancer, Wyatt Hunt made time to drive him to the hospital in Safford for chemo. Dad said Hunt alone helped Manny Vasquez with chores and rounding up and selling his herd. If for no other reason, *that* would convince me to rent a casita to the wildlife biologist again." In a last show of defiance she squared her shoulders, took Scotty by the hand and marched them to an exit door she stiff-armed open.

"You're making a big mistake," Hicks called.

"Stick it where the sun don't shine!"

Whatever else he may have shouted back got cut off by the slam of the heavy door behind Tandy.

She half carried her gangly son to the parking lot, where she unlocked and wrenched open the back door to her SUV. She lifted him into his booster seat, helped him buckle up and hugged him when he started to cry. "Shh. I won't let them hurt us."

"I don't like that bad man with the big shiny belt buckle. He hollered at you. I wanna go back to Honolulu and live with my cousins."

Tandy's heart sank. "Oh, Scotty, the ranch is our home now." She gently shut his door and rounded the hood to slide behind the wheel. She glanced back at him before jamming the key in the ignition of the aging Wagoneer that had belonged to her dad.

"What's a wolf man?" Scotty asked, wiping his sniffling nose on his sleeve. "Is he like a werewolf?"

"Heavens, no. Werewolves are folklore. They aren't real." Tandy wrenched too hard on the key and the Jeep roared to life then sputtered and died. "Where did you hear about werewolves anyway?"

"From Mark. He's got a cool movie."

"Auntie Lucinda let you kids watch that kind of thing?"

"Uh-huh. And vampires, too. And zombies."

"Sheesh. Well, Mr. Hunt is a regular man. He'll be renting the casita next to Manny's for a month starting tomorrow, and he's one member of a team of wildlife biologists who brought Mexican gray wolves back into this area while your grandpa was alive."

"Cool." Scotty swept his hand across his eyes, drying his tears.

"As I understand it, Mr. Hunt needs to track those wolves, count their pups then vaccinate and tag them for a wildlife project."

"But that man shouldn't have been mean to you. I hope the wolf man's nicer. Is he?"

"Please call him Mr. Hunt. Grandpa Marsh liked him a lot and spoke highly of him whenever we talked. Manny says good things about Mr. Hunt, too."

"If he's not nice I'll have Mr. Bones bite him," Scotty said, brightening considerably the minute he mentioned the Redbone Coonhound. She'd gotten him from the local animal shelter in hopes of helping ease Scotty's transition to life on a ranch.

"We don't want Mr. Bones biting anyone." Tandy loosened her grip on the key and this time started the vehicle without incident. She couldn't help smiling to herself at her son's protective instincts. However, her smile soon faded. At thirty-one, she was plagued by plenty of mixed feelings over her abrupt but necessary departure from the military, where she'd enjoyed her job and had earned a steady paycheck.

Scotty had no clue how their lives had changed when his dad, also an army sergeant, had phoned to say he'd fallen in love with another woman. Dan was stationed in the Philippines while she'd served in Afghanistan. Hearing long-distance that he wanted a divorce had stung. But when he had angrily insisted he'd never wanted kids, leaving the army for the ranch she'd inherited in Arizona had seemed the only choice for her and Scotty.

Cutting ties in Hawaii had been necessary because Dan's sister, Lucinda, had cared for Scotty while both parents were deployed. She'd said to keep the peace in her family, she had to side with her brother. Compared to all that, having a group of old ranchers attempting to bully her felt minor.

Checking her son in the rearview mirror, it hurt seeing his tear-stained face. Back when she'd first learned she was pregnant, not long after hers and Dan's whirlwind romance, he had mentioned not wanting kids. She should've divorced him then. And would have if he hadn't sweet-talked her into believing he'd spoken in the heat of the moment. Only during the divorce had she learned he'd been up for a promotion at the time. So, the jackass's change of heart had been because his CO wouldn't have promoted him if he'd thought Dan would dump a pregnant wife.

She rolled down her window to let a breeze cool her anger. She should've said more to those ranchers. Like she ought to have seen through Dan. Oh, but why replow old ground? It was probably a godsend their jobs had kept them apart. Now she was well rid of him.

Still, she felt bad for Scotty. He missed his aunt and cousins. He wasn't as happy with their move to the ranch as Tandy had hoped. She wished she had more hours each day to spend being his mom. But boning up on raising cattle and building a herd demanded a lot of time.

And they could use the income from renting a casita to Wyatt Hunt. While it'd been a blessing to inherit Spiritridge, most of the funds in her father's bank account went to clearing his medical bills. She'd tapped her savings for the move and to buy cattle. And her dad's elderly ranch hand, who she was happy had agreed to work for her, had been very frank about how long it'd take her to turn a profit with a fledgling herd. Especially since she hadn't yet purchased a bull to turn out with her heifers.

Maybe she should've sold the ranch. At the time she just wanted to escape rejection and go where she'd been blessed to have had an idyllic childhood. That carefree life was what she wanted for Scotty. And by damn, she wouldn't let angry, futzy old ranchers like Preston Hicks and his minions wreck that.

THE NEXT MORNING, Tandy looked out her kitchen window and saw thick fog rolling over the basin. The white mist completely shrouded the usually dark Santa Teresa and craggy Galiuro Mountains that ringed the high desert where she ran her cattle.

She let the kitchen curtain drop and filled her coffee mug, further worrying they might get snow today. She'd turned her calendar to February, but having grown up here she knew it could snow as late as April.

"Mama, do we hafta go feed cows? I'm cold," Scotty said, yawning and rubbing his eyes as he came into the kitchen.

Mr. Bones padded after him; his dog tags clinked merrily as he trotted around the boy and went straight to his dish of kibble, which Tandy had already set out.

"We do, Scotty," she said as he took his seat at the kitchen table. "Raising cattle is pretty much an all-day, every day job. But I'll ask Manny if we can start later. See if this fog burns off a bit. Wear one of the flannel shirts we bought, and the lined denim jacket. If you'd like, you can ride with me on Butterscotch. If you sit in front of me, I'll block most of the chilly wind."

"Nah, I'll ride Patch," he said, referencing the small, sure-footed mule his grandfather's longtime ranch hand had found for him. "I don't want Mr. Manny to think I'm a sissy," Scotty declared as he dug into the bowl of hot cereal Tandy had set before him.

"A sissy? Honestly, Scotty, if your cousin taught you that, I'm triply glad we left Hawaii to live here."

"Mark knows everything. He's in fourth grade, you know."

Tandy stifled a laugh. She might have said more except her cell phone rang. She hurried to the counter, where it sat on its charger.

"Maybe that'll be the wolf man calling to say he's coming today." Scotty perked right up.

"It's Manny," Tandy said, seeing her cowhand's name on the screen. She picked up the phone and put it to her ear. "Manny, hi. We'll be ready to ride shortly. We're running a little late. I'm considering waiting until this fog burns off some to go out. Will that be okay with you?"

"Fine, Tandy. This weather is playing havoc with my arthritic joints. I hope you can handle checking stock today without me."

"I'll have to. Do you have medication? Is there anything you need?"

"I'm good. This damp snap wasn't predicted. I do

okay if I have a couple days' warning so I can start taking a heavy-duty analgesic."

Tandy had feared Manny's advanced age might be an issue. She relied on him because he'd been loyal to her father, and he'd offered his help. "I'm sorry your joints hurt," she murmured. "I'll take my cell phone if you need me. Otherwise, I'll give you a call when Scotty and I finish for the day. Better yet, I'll bring you supper."

"Thanks, I'd like that. By the way, how was the association meeting last night? What was their big emergency?"

"Ah, the meeting. It was called to do a hatchet job on me. Preston Hicks tore into me for renting a casita to Wyatt Hunt. I wouldn't have thought so many grown men could throw fits over a few wolves. Wolves lived here before ranchers moved in."

She handed Scotty a piece of toast to go with his cereal and broke off a corner of a second slice for herself.

"Steer clear of Hicks," the old man warned. "He led the association to band together against Wyatt when he and his team released the wolves. Somebody, and your pa thought it was Pres, laid a dead wolf on the hood of Wyatt's vehicle as a threat. He and others on his team got phone threats, too. But the government agency in charge of the wolf program sent out a letter saying whoever did it could be prosecuted."

"I wish I'd known all of that before I agreed to rent to Mr. Hunt. New as I am, I don't need to be the source of grief to neighbors. I also don't like being stuck in the middle of a turf war over wolf repatriation."

"Your pa favored the program. He told Hunt to ignore Preston's bluster. Best you avoid them if you can, Tandy."

"I know Dad liked Mr. Hunt a lot. I promise not to go out of my way to engage Hicks. But I won't cower, either. You take care of your arthritis. If you need groceries or anything from town, I hope to make a run to the feed store tomorrow or the next day."

"I'm good, but thanks. With luck I'll be back in the saddle tomorrow."

She ended their call, sighed and put away her phone.

"What's wrong?" Scotty asked.

"Manny can't ride with us today. He has an illness called arthritis that causes him pain in his knees, elbows and fingers. He believes he'll feel better tomorrow."

"I heard that. He talks really loud. But what did he say about a dead wolf? How did one die, Mama?"

"It's nothing for us to worry about. It didn't happen recently."

"You sounded worried. Is it 'cause that bad man said don't rent to the wolf man?"

"Honey, he was making noise. I don't want you to be concerned. Please call him Mr. Hunt. If you're finished with your cereal, rinse the bowl then go get dressed. You can watch TV while I fix something in advance for supper. We'll let the fog lift before we go feed cattle."

Scotty slipped off his chair and carried his bowl to the sink. "Can we have pa'sketti?"

"*Spa*ghetti." Tandy stressed the correct pronunciation.

"Yeah, that's what I said."

Laughing, Tandy tweaked his cowlick. "I can make that. Outside of pizza I know it's your most favorite food."

"Yup. If the wolf man, uh, Mr. Hunt, comes today like the bad man said, he can eat supper with us and tell us all about the wolves."

"No, Scotty. He's only renting one of our casitas. He will cook his own meals. I doubt we'll see much of him at all. I hope anyway," she added under her breath.

"Aww, I wanna see his baby wolves."

"Forget that. We want all wolves to stay far away from the ranch."

"Me and Mr. Bones could take care of a baby wolf, dontcha think?"

"Not a good plan." Tandy shooed him and the hound out of the kitchen.

SOME TWELVE HOURS after they'd had their morning discussion and rehashed it several times, Tandy and Scotty rode back to the barn. It'd been a hard day because the fog hadn't lifted until midafternoon and hung in the deeper arroyos where she'd needed to check on cows and fill water troughs. Scotty had driven her crazy by constantly riding his mule off into underbrush, claiming to be searching for wolf cubs.

Unsaddling Butterscotch, and then Patch, she wondered what had made her think she could chase a herd of Santa Gertrudis cattle over an inhospitable landscape, take care of a house, and maybe homeschool her almost-six-year-old son in the fall when he began first grade. Maybe because her mother had done the same until Tandy started third grade.

"Hurry, Mama. I'm starved and so is Mr. Bones." Scotty called to her from the fading light outside the barn door.

"I'm coming. But you're going to have to give me time to fix garlic bread and a salad while the spaghetti heats through."

Scotty skipped ahead with his pet. Tandy lagged behind. She'd assumed all the patrols she'd led over rough terrain in Afghanistan would have prepared her to chase after and feed a few hundred cows. Obviously not. She was exhausted.

"Honey, why don't you build something with your Legos while supper warms? I'll bring Manny his plate first. I hope he's not feeling worse, now that the fog has settled again."

Scotty stopped at the front door and glanced around. "It's almost dark and the wolf man hasn't come. Do you think that bad guy from last night shot him?"

"Scotty!" Tandy gasped his name as she reached around him and turned on the interior lights. "Area ranchers may not want him here, but no one would go that far."

"They might," he said, trudging down the hall. "Didn't you see? The bad man had a gun."

She hadn't noticed. She worried that Scotty had

heard too much violent war-talk, living with an uncle in the navy, as well as his dad and herself.

She headed to the kitchen and in about forty minutes the meal was ready. But she hadn't taken time to clean up. She still felt grungy from a full day of herding strays out of canyons. Oh, well, she'd shower before bed.

"Scotty, come eat. The garlic bread is due out in a minute."

She heard him leave his room just as the doorbell rang.

"I'll answer the door, Mama."

"Okay. It's probably Manny. Tell him I'll fix that plate, or better, he should come eat with us." She tore off a piece of foil to cover the dish if he didn't elect to stay. He'd said often the hired help shouldn't eat with the boss. Silly as it sounded to her, apparently he'd been that way until her father got sick and needed assistance preparing his meals.

The oven timer dinged. She slipped on oven mitts to remove the casserole dish and the hot bread.

From the other room a male voice she didn't recognize said, "Hi there, young man. I'm here to pick up a key to one of the casitas from Ms. Graham. Is that your mother?"

"Are you the wolf man?" Scotty exclaimed, his tone filled with awe. "Mama's in the kitchen putting pa'sketti on the table. It's super yummy. Come on in and eat with us."

Tandy almost dropped the bread. In the middle of finding a place to set the hot item she heard the man laugh. It was a deep rumble that reminded her of how disheveled she looked. Her free hand flew to smooth down her hair. Not wanting her first meeting with her renter to put her at a disadvantage for wearing grubby jeans and a sauce-spattered work shirt, she called to Scotty. "His house key is on the end table beside the lamp."

Before she could add that the casita was stocked and ready, she heard their new tenant saying how the food certainly smelled good.

Considering the lateness of the hour, the poor man had probably been traveling through the fog instead of stopping to eat. Having a change of heart for someone who'd been a friend to her dad, she stepped to the arch and almost fell over Mr. Bones. "Scotty, show him where to wash up. I'll set another plate."

Tandy rushed back and set out another place setting. She was tearing off extra paper towel for napkins when her son, jabbering a mile a minute, dragged their guest into the kitchen. Glancing up, a welcoming smile froze on her lips, and the paper towel fluttered from her hand. She and the newcomer both grabbed for it, causing their hands to connect. The strength in his fingers sent shock waves rippling up Tandy's arm. She quickly withdrew, leaving him to catch the towel before it hit the floor.

Wyatt Hunt was nothing like she'd presumed. For one thing, he was a lot younger. And gosh, he was tall. Over six feet, she judged. Wide shouldered and narrow hipped, he wore cowboy garb as if it'd been tailor-made to fit his muscular frame. His dark blond hair showed a stubborn curl. When he smiled down at Scotty, a dimple flashed in his left cheek.

His good looks sent Tandy's heart thudding like a jungle drum. She felt even more rattled when considering again how crappy she must look.

But the unexpected weakness that attacked her knees annoyed her. Good grief, she'd worked with, and had outranked, more handsome men than him. What was wrong with her? "Sorry to stare, but I'd assumed from conversations with Dad that you were his age," she blurted even as her son urged the man to sit in the chair beside him. "He never actually mentioned your age during our phone calls, but it was an impression he gave in how he talked about views you two shared."

"Curt and I hit it off, but he was what…sixtyish? Twice my age. Is this where you'd like me to sit?" he asked Tandy, pointing to the chair Scotty kept urging him toward. "Are you sure I'm not putting you out?"

"Oh, no. I feel as if I know you. You were so good to Dad. Scotty, let him fill his plate first. I'm going to take this one over to Manny. His arthritis is acting up," she told Wyatt, who also knew the other man.

"Ask him if there's anything I can do to help," Wyatt said after sitting down. "Carry in wood for his fireplace or something. Or if you'd like, I'll take him the plate." He started to rise again.

"That's not necessary." Tandy deftly covered the plate with foil. "I'll ask about the wood. You two tear off bread slices while it's hot."

She dashed out and was gone only a few minutes. Returning, pretty much out of breath, she scooted around the narrow table and took a seat directly across from their guest. When her knees bumped Wyatt's, he didn't seem to notice.

"How is Manny doing? I'm sorry his joints aren't any better than they were during the roundup I helped him with last year."

"He appreciated the food and your offer. He swears he's better, though, and will ride with us tomorrow," Tandy said, putting a scoop of spaghetti on Scotty's plate.

"All of this looks so good." Wyatt eyed the offerings as if it was a feast.

"Uh, help yourself." Tandy scooted the casserole dish toward him. She took a deep and deliberate breath before serving up salad for her son. And she followed that with a squirt of dressing for the boy, who continued to gaze rapturously at their unplanned guest as if he'd never shared a supper table with a grown man before. It probably had been a while, Tandy thought.

"I'm not the greatest cook," she mumbled, then didn't know why she had felt a need to say anything.

Wyatt glanced up from his full plate and smiled at her. "You could've fooled me. I've only had a taste, but spaghetti is a favorite of mine, and garlic bread hits the spot."

Scotty beamed. "Mama fixed it 'cause it's my favorite next to pizza, which she can't make," he added.

Tandy filled her plate. "Knowing Dad, he probably told you I went into the army after college. There we always had cooks or ate MREs. I hoped I'd have more time to spend with cookbooks after moving back here. Turns out I have a lot to learn about raising cattle. Maybe things won't be so hectic after we acquire a full herd."

"It's a shame we had to sell all of Curt's cattle after he passed so suddenly. I grew up in cattle country, so I know herds build slowly."

"I've bought a decent amount of heifers. Manny's looking for a bull to round out my stock. So far, no luck." She frowned and rolled noodles around her fork. "After the stockmen's meeting last night, it's a toss-up whether anyone will sell me anything. Are you aware local ranchers are unhappy with me for renting you a casita?"

"I'm sorry. I might've guessed, considering how many reacted poorly when we began this project." The man shred his bread. "I'll make other arrangements and move elsewhere. No sense in you taking flak."

"You can't go away." Scotty stopped eating. "There was a bad man at the meeting who yelled at my mom. He's scary. I'm glad you aren't old like Manny 'cause you can punch him if he acts mean again."

"Scotty." Tandy shook her head. "No one's going to punch Mr. Hicks. Fighting isn't how we solve our differences."

"But Auntie Lucinda said…" Whatever he'd been about to say withered under his mother's stern glare.

Wyatt gazed briefly at the upset boy before returning his attention to Tandy. "Often it only takes one disgruntled person to stir up mob mentality. Area ranchers have all been informed that our agency will pay double for any cattle they can prove our wolf pack brought down. I don't like hearing they're still so upset. To date we haven't had a single confirmed incident."

"Dad favored repatriation of the Mexican gray wolves to this area. I recall him telling me the elk population had exploded and they were ruining the range grass where he grazed cattle."

"True. He might've been the only local rancher who understood the Game and Fish program. By the time my team mapped this area and chose the best spot to release two wolf pair, Curt was too ill to attend any of our meetings. I hope no one harassed him. If they did, he never told me."

Tandy shook her head. "I don't think they did. Last night, Preston Hicks said as much. My parents were well liked. Dad kept ranching a long time after my mom died. Apparently I'm a different story. But I don't push around easily. Besides, you and I have an agreement. I'm fully prepared to honor it."

Wyatt nodded and ate a few bites.

"Me and Mama want you to stay. I've only seen wolves on the TV," Scotty said. "Wolves look like dogs. Why don't people like them? I wish I knew more about 'em."

"How old are you?" Wyatt asked, pausing to study the boy.

Scotty puffed out his chest. "I'm gonna be six pretty soon. In March. But I already know the alphabet and I can count to a thousand."

"Good for you. I thought you were older," Hunt said and grinned. "The state Game and Fish Department has informational pamphlets we give to schools on the different varieties of wolves. There's more reading than photographs, though." He considered for a moment. "I know there's a library in town. I'd be happy to see if they have any books on wolves for younger kids during my next supply run. That is, if your mom has no objection." He shifted his gaze to Tandy.

"You don't care, do you, Mama? A book on wolves would be so cool. It'd be even cooler to see a real live wolf. Then I could phone Mark, and he'd want to come visit me."

Tandy choked on a cherry tomato she'd bit into. "Scotty. Hawaii is a long way from Arizona. Airplane flights are costly." She didn't want to tell him that his aunt might not welcome having Scotty invite Mark to Arizona. Which was a shame since the divorce was all at the feet of Lucinda's brother.

Seeing her son's face cloud, Tandy quickly said, "Let's see if Mr. Hunt can find a suitable book, Scotty. Then we'll talk about you getting in touch with Mark."

"Please, if you don't mind, both of you call me Wyatt. Mr. Hunt is too formal."

Tandy nodded at Scotty to show it was okay with her, then added, "We call Manny by his first name."

"Okay, *Wyatt*," Scotty said with a grin. Wyatt winked at her son.

"Finish before your spaghetti gets cold. And stop feeding Mr. Bones the mushrooms you're picking out."

Scotty's eyes snapped open. "Sorry," he mumbled. "I don't like 'shrooms."

Tandy smothered a smile. "Neither does Mr.

Bones. He's spit them all out on the floor. So just push them to one side of your plate. And be careful where you step when you leave the table."

She noticed Wyatt's blue eyes sparkled with humor, giving Tandy another twist in her stomach, a reaction similar to when she'd heard him laugh. That had been extraweird since the last thing she was in the market for was a romantic relationship. If falling so hard and fast for Dan had taught her anything, it was how unreliable her heart was. Plus, she didn't want to get involved with another man who traveled for work.

For the remainder of the meal, between bites, Scotty shot questions about wolves at Wyatt. He asked why so many people didn't like them. He asked what they ate. And if it hurt wolf pups to get vaccinations. "I don't like needles," he said.

What amazed Tandy was how Wyatt didn't brush her son off. Instead he patiently answered every question in language appropriate for his age. That wasn't anything Scotty's own father or his uncle would've done. She'd seen them ignore or send away Scotty and his three cousins.

By the end of the meal Scotty had begun to yawn. "It's time we let Wyatt go check out his casita, and you, young man, need to get ready for bed while I clean off the table." She stood and began stacking plates.

"The meal was great," Wyatt said, folding his paper towel napkin. "Let me help with dishes."

His offer was nothing Tandy expected or was used to. Even out in the field, a lot of guys in uniform assumed the females in their squadron would naturally take on all domestic chores. "If you want to carry your plate to the sink, I'll fetch your key. I did make the bed up over there and set towels in the bathroom. Manny handles his own laundry. Am I correct to assume you'll do the same?"

"I will. I brought bedding. But thanks for readying the place. I had a morning meeting in Albuquerque so I drove straight through, not wanting to roust you from your bed to get the key. I tried calling the house. You must've been out with the cattle. That reminds me, can we exchange cell numbers before I leave?"

"Sure."

"Me'n Mr. Bones are going to bed. G'night, Mom. G'night, Wyatt. I hope you find me a wolf book." The boy threw his arms around the legs of the man he'd only recently met and gave him a good-night hug before he hugged his mother.

She watched boy and dog lope noisily down the tiled hallway and waited until she was sure Scotty had gone into his room before they traded numbers. She handed Wyatt the casita key, murmuring, "Thank you for not dismissing Scotty's questions out of hand. But I don't want him becoming a bother. I've noticed since we moved here how curious he is about everything. Even I tune him out at times, and I'm sure my ex-husband did, too." She shepherded the tall man to the front door.

"Ex-husband?" he said unexpectedly. "Uh, sorry if that sounded rude. Curt didn't know you were contemplating divorce, did he? I…ah…probably shouldn't say anything." Wyatt seemed embarrassed. "He lamented never hearing from his son-in-law. Not even when he was most sick. Manny said it probably wasn't easy to get calls out from a war zone, but you managed a couple of calls a week. I remember thinking it especially odd since Curt said your husband was stationed in the Philippines."

Tandy opened the door and clung to it while Wyatt shrugged into his jacket.

"Look, tell me to stop being nosy. But, I thought the world of your father. He treated me like a son. Stuff that worried him worried me. I'm sure you had good reason for not telling him if your marriage was in trouble." Wyatt crossed the porch. "Thanks again for the terrific meal. Uh, would you rather I conveniently not find a kid's book on wolves?" He hesitated at the steps and leveled an uneasy gaze on Tandy.

"A kid wolf book would be great. But, just to clarify, my marriage ended abruptly after Dad died. I truly appreciate all you did for him. I hope you don't think I'm horrible for not coming home for his funeral. I tried to get leave, but the fighting in Afghanistan had heated up and nonessential flights from our base were grounded without exception. I so regret that." She smudged away an errant tear. "You'd left by the time I finally managed to make it home."

Wyatt shook his head. "I didn't think you were horrible. Fortunately your dad had prearranged his funeral. The funeral home in town carried out his wishes for a private service. Manny and I attended. We both understood why you couldn't be here."

"Thanks. Manny said as much, but it helps to hear you agree. About the book for Scotty, please don't go out of your way to find one. I know you must be on a schedule."

"In case you couldn't tell, I love educating anyone who'll listen about ensuring wolf habitats remain as nature intended. I'll keep the book age appropriate. I hope I can find one with photos." Giving a final wave, Wyatt descended the steps.

Tandy heard him whistling as he crossed the sandy yard to the casita next to Manny's. It wasn't until she saw lights spill from his door and windows that she realized she still stood in the cold after she could no longer see and admire the man's lithe stride.

Chapter Two

The first morning after his return to the ranch, Wyatt stood at the front window of his casita, drinking coffee and watching daylight blossom over the mountain rim. Tandy had not only readied his bed and bathroom, she'd left a pound of Kona coffee beside the coffee maker. He'd never drunk Hawaiian coffee, but it was quite good. He'd have to remember to thank her.

All at once his eyes were drawn away from the streaky salmon glow in the east to the boy he'd met the previous night. Scotty Graham chased after his dog, heading toward the barn. On his heels was his mother, all decked out in boots, jeans, a plaid jacket and a ski cap with earflaps. She caught up to her son, grabbed him around the waist and stuffed him into a denim jacket with a hood that from all appearances he didn't want to wear. The scene made Wyatt smile.

Pausing with his lips on his mug, he realized how much there was to admire about his new landlady. More than her curly brown hair and dark chocolate eyes. Even more than her trim body, although it certainly lit a few fires in his belly. Just now, instead of scolding her recalcitrant son, her pretty face was filled with love and laughter.

Wyatt imagined the trilling sound and the thought marched fingers of unexpected heat up his spine. His imagination was cut short when Manny Vasquez hobbled on bowlegs to join the others, and the trio continued on into the barn.

Wyatt's first order of business today was to follow a hiking trail beyond a campground, looking for signs that his wolves had traveled lower in bad weather in search of easier prey. He hoped not, because that was when they could trouble ranchers.

Later in the day he'd go to town for supplies. Wyatt actually wished he didn't have to make either trip. He'd like to saddle a horse and ride with the others through quiet canyons where cattle roamed. He'd had a taste of that when he'd helped Tandy's father and recalled he'd rather enjoyed the ranch routine.

Turning from the window, he drained his first cup of java and poured another in a travel mug. He spared a moment, feeling glad that Tandy had been aware he'd bonded with her dad in the year spent here establishing his wolf project. His parents, busy, dedicated archaeologists, rarely found time to connect or ask about his work, as they were so focused on their own.

The fact Curtis Marsh had been so ill may've been why he'd welcomed Wyatt's company. Or maybe the man knew his end was near and he profoundly missed his only child. Because he sometimes got lonely, too, Wyatt had enjoyed hearing of the man's unabashed love for his deceased wife and his pride for his daughter, who had served multiple tours in war-torn Iraq and Afghanistan.

Tandy's father had worried about her. Curt wished she'd come home and bring his grandson. Due to their chats, Wyatt guessed he might know Tandy better than she knew him. He'd pored over family photos, from the time she was born to her college graduation to when she finally wore an army uniform. Oddly there were no wedding pictures and very few of her and her son, which made Curt cherish every one.

Ah, well, until last evening Wyatt hadn't known she'd divorced. Capping his travel mug, he told himself that detail didn't matter. Shouldn't matter. Couldn't matter. Similar to her army deployments, Game and Fish sent him far afield on assignments. Many were remote locations. He used to like that part of his job. Still, it could get old.

Donning his jacket and backpack filled with gear, he set out for the hills where he might find wolf tracks.

By 11:00 a.m. he'd tramped from the highway along two well-traveled trails. Both bordered Spiritidge land. The last one he wanted to check passed nearer to Preston Hicks's ranch. At a point where the trail curved and dipped for a mile, it ran alongside a popular summer campground.

More than halfway to higher ground by noon, Wyatt thought he heard a tiny bit of static coming through his tracking device. That meant one of his banded adult wolves was in the area. He hiked on, listening carefully, checking all around for tracks or scat.

The static faded. He reached a wide mesa without seeing any evidence of wolves, for which he was thankful. Next time out he'd climb higher to where helicopter spotters had last seen the pack during the winter. Newly released wolves often traveled a great distance from where they were let go. Being smart animals, it was thought they could smell the cage long after it'd been removed. Mostly they steered clear of the smell of man, too.

He circled back toward the ranch. He'd only gone a hundred yards or so when, out of the corner of one eye, he glimpsed the furry backsides of two animals. He lifted his binoculars for a clearer look but saw nothing. Must have been the twitch of a branch, but no wind had come up to rustle across the countryside.

He left the trail to look for tracks in the underbrush. Twice more he saw a brief flash of fur but failed to get close enough to snap a picture with his camera. The animals resembled full-grown wolves. Yet he wasn't picking up feedback on his scanner. That meant they weren't his wolves.

A dozen feet off the trail he spotted half a paw print. It could be from a wolf, or a big dog. He knelt, letting his brain sort through possibilities. This was a fair distance from any ranch house. If the dogs were sheepherders, he'd think they would come to him instead of running away.

He scraped debris away from the print and took the best photo he could manage. Not finding additional tracks, he literally crawled along, hoping to run across more.

Before his team had scouted this area, another wildlife management group gave a workshop on wolf dogs. Hybrids could crop up several years after a re-patriation, especially near ranching communities. But his team's release hadn't been long enough ago for either of their alphas to mate with dogs and produce offspring the size of the animals he'd sighted.

So, what did it mean? Could strays have crossed over the mountains from New Mexico? Their release had been a while ago. Long enough that those wolves no longer wore radio collars.

Traveling deeper into an almost impenetrable thicket, Wyatt hit a wall of vines, gave up and turned back. There were no further sightings of creatures other than a rabbit and a few flitting birds. And his wolves weren't here.

Heading to the ranch, he considered calling Tandy before going to town. Last night he should've asked if there was anything he could pick up for her or Manny.

As it turned out, he didn't have phone reception until he was back at his casita. He unloaded equipment from his official SUV and tried Tandy before leaving. She might be out of satellite range. He wondered if she was aware of how spotty phone service was where she ran cattle.

The call connected and he heard her faint "Hello."

"Hi, Tandy, it's Wyatt. I'm ready to run into town. Is there anything I can pick up for you, or if Manny's with you, anything I can get for him?"

"It's nice of you to ask, but we're on our back forty, so I'm not able to give you a list or money."

"No problem. Tell me what you need. We can settle up later."

"Mainly I need milk, eggs and dog food." She named the kind of kibble she bought for Mr. Bones.

Wyatt heard her ask if Manny would like him to pick up anything.

"Liniment," she said a moment later.

"Okay, got it. If you think of anything else, give me a ring. Say, I just had a thought. I know a pizza place that sells premade, uncooked pizzas. How about I grab a couple and feed you and Scotty tonight? What toppings?"

"You don't have to do that. He's asking me to remind you about a library book on wolves. And he wants to know if you found your wolf pups?"

"Tell him I won't forget the book. And I didn't locate my wolf packs. I picked up a faint signal once on my tracking device, but it didn't prove to be solid."

Wyatt would have to find out if Tandy knew of any hybrids in the area. Or maybe he'd ask Manny first. He didn't want to cause her any concern about wolf dogs, which could be meaner than wild wolves.

"I hope to be back before dark. About those pizzas... do you want me to choose toppings?"

"If you insist on picking some up, we'd love that. Scotty's favorite is pepperoni. I like any form that passes for Hawaiian with pineapple and pork. But I could eat whatever you like. Really, I'm not fussy. Oh, can you hear Scotty chanting pizza, pizza, pizza? It's truly his most favorite food. I should make him do veggie."

Tandy's laughter was the exact melodious sound Wyatt had imagined about earlier. "Tell him it'll be a while." Wyatt chuckled. "I'll see you both later. I actually know what toppings Manny likes. Tell him I'll bring him a small sausage, mushroom and dried tomato." He heard the man call out his thanks. Still smiling over the exchange, which gave him an inclusive feeling like he'd enjoyed with Curt before he'd passed, Wyatt said goodbye and drove away.

He'd reached the outskirts of town where most locals shopped when he decided he'd rather buy Scotty a book that he could keep instead of getting one he'd have to return to the library. He recalled passing a bookstore during the many times he'd taken Curt for chemo treatments to the next larger town.

He figured he could go there and still have time to come back for groceries and pizzas.

Once he reached Safford, he went straight to the bookstore. He actually wasn't sure if he'd find any children's books on wolves or wolf families.

Much to his surprise, there was one with great photographs. Heading to check out, he spotted an endcap of posters. One jumped out: three wolves lying under a tree. Two adults and a pup. From their coloring and the high mountains rising in the background, they could be Mexican grays from the Arizona project or New Mexico. Hoping Tandy would let Scotty hang the poster, he added it to the book. While in line, he saw a new mystery by an author he liked and grabbed it.

As his work was so solitary, most evenings he read. Usually he had agency material or wildlife magazines. But he did like intrigue mixed with adventure.

As he paid for his purchases, Wyatt wondered if Tandy liked to read, and if so, what she preferred? He hadn't met any women who'd been in the military.

And according to Curt, she'd commanded a combat support team. What made her choose that life? It seemed harsher than most careers.

He knew quite a few women who worked with wildlife. That could be hard, too. He'd dated a park ranger until she'd transferred to a job in the Northwest.

After pocketing his credit card, he collected his package and left the store. He hadn't thought about Kylie Porter in a while. Their relationship hadn't stood up under long distance. His job came first. Still, it bothered him when Kylie accused him of being like his parents who'd never owned a home and were always off on wilderness digs. During his younger years, he'd lived in Las Cruces, New Mexico, with his maternal grandmother.

Now the closest thing he had to a permanent residence was the cabin he often stayed in on a cattle ranch near Silver City. His best friend, Loki Branchwater, owned the ranch. Wyatt was so steeped in thought he drove straight past the general store. When it dawned on him, he made a U-turn and went back. He breezed through the store, loading his cart with items Tandy and Manny had requested. Then he added things from his list.

He didn't pass anyone in the aisles he knew, which was fine since Tandy had said he wasn't popular. He checked out quickly with his mind on picking up the pizzas.

The minute he unlocked his vehicle he noticed a series of deep gouges through the paint on his front and back doors. The strips tore jaggedly through the Game and Fish logo.

For a moment he only gaped at the vandalism. Then he glanced around to see if the person or persons responsible lurked nearby. He'd heard of automobiles being keyed, but until now he'd never seen what damage it could do. There were a few cars in the lot, but no one visible.

It could've been kids. A check of his watch showed it wasn't quite three, so the high school and junior high wouldn't be out.

As he unloaded the cart, he had little doubt that he'd been deliberately targeted. Possibly by an irate rancher.

After returning the cart to the front of the store, he drove to the sheriff's office. In the past, local authorities partnered with Game and Fish to back teams if anyone instigated mischief of the type that had just occurred.

Sheriff Doug Anderson manned the office alone. He looked up from his computer when Wyatt walked in. The silver-haired man immediately stood and extended a hand. "Say there, Hunt, I heard you were going to spend time with us again. I'll tell you what I told a contingent of ranchers—my deputies and I have enough to do. We don't need a hullabaloo blowing up over you wildlife guys."

Wyatt disengaged his hand. "I've only been back one day. I stopped at the general store for supplies. While I was inside, someone raked a key to hell and gone across the driver's side of my government SUV.

I came straight here, so I'm guessing it happened between half an hour and forty-five minutes ago."

The sheriff sank back in his swivel chair. "Dammit all. Were there any eyewitnesses?"

"There were maybe four cars and a couple of pickups in the lot. That pretty much matches the number of shoppers I saw in the store. No one I knew or who acted as if they knew me. The parking lot itself was empty of people except for me."

Anderson yanked open a drawer and pulled out a pad of preprinted pages. He tore one off and passed it to Wyatt. "This is an official complaint form. While you fill it out, I'll go take pictures of the damage. Are you parked in front of my office?"

Wyatt nodded. "I'll fill it out, for all the good it'll do. No witnesses and probably no fingerprints. That's the thing about key damage, hard to identify who held the key." His face turned sour. "If you want my best guess, it'd be Preston Hicks or Jim Haskell."

The sheriff paused. "Why them? Both have been pillars of this community for decades."

"Yeah, well, they and a few others deviled my team last year. If you recall, we never were sure who left a dead wolf on the hood of my SUV."

"We exhausted all our leads on that one." The sheriff raised an eyebrow. "You working with your team this time?"

"I'm alone this trip. Came to check on our packs—count pups, install radio collars and vaccinate them. I'm renting again at Spiritridge Ranch. This time from Curt Marsh's daughter. She mentioned taking heat at a cattle and sheep rancher's meeting. Hicks apparently led a rant against me."

"This is the first I've heard of issues at the meeting. I've seen Curt's daughter and her son around town. If Pres gave her grief, why didn't she report it to me?"

Wyatt shrugged. "I don't know. She is ex-army. I don't think she's easily intimidated."

"I remember as a teenager she was a tough competitor in a couple of sports."

"Doesn't surprise me. What did she play?"

"Hmm. Maybe softball, and track and field events."

Wyatt could tell the sheriff was combing his memory. "It doesn't matter. I don't want guys who are PO'd at me picking on her or the boy. He's sort of fearless, too." *It's remarkable, really, for as young as Scotty is.*

The sheriff waved his phone. "I'll go take those photos while you complete the form as best you can. I know you didn't see the incident, but an approximate time and place is important if my deputies are out asking casual questions."

"Speaking of casual questions," Wyatt called to the man about ready to walk out the door, "have you heard of any wolf dogs in the vicinity?"

"Wolf dogs? What are they?"

"Mostly a shepherd-type dog bred with a wolf. They carry features of both, but the ones I've seen in our lecture films are larger and meaner than a domestic dog."

"Huh. I haven't heard of anything like that around.

I doubt they'd survive long with all our cattle and sheep ranchers. They'd be trapped or shot."

"Trapped?" Wyatt looked up sharply from the paper he'd started to read. "What kind? Claw traps are outlawed and others require a license."

"Don't get all riled up." Scowling, the sheriff crossed his arms. "I don't know if anybody's using traps. Used to be some ranches had trouble with mountain cats. I know someone built and set a box trap near their chicken coop. Caught the cat and called Game and Fish to take him away. That was probably four years ago. If your boss has been over this area that long, he'd likely remember the case."

"He covers this project and a few others. I have to call him about the SUV. I'll ask about traps."

The sheriff went on outside and Wyatt filled out the form.

Sheriff Anderson returned, printed the photo off and clipped it to the report he had Wyatt sign and date. They shook hands and Wyatt left to go order pizzas. He'd spent longer than anticipated with the sheriff. He hoped the side trip wouldn't make him so late that Tandy would give up on him and cook supper.

The owner of the pizza shop recognized him but didn't really know who he was. The man mentioned he hadn't seen Wyatt in a while, when he used to be a regular.

"I've been out of town for my job," he said, not wanting to draw attention to himself lest anyone in the establishment not be happy to see him back.

While his take-and-bake order was in progress he

stepped outside to call his boss. He currently headed a five-state wolf repatriation program.

"Is the hostility bad enough you want to be pulled from the area?" his leader asked after hearing Wyatt's story.

"I wasn't threatened, Joe. It may have been kids, although I doubt it." He relayed what had happened to Tandy at the rancher's meeting. "I want to continue."

"Good. We have some of our Mesquite pack dead down in the Chiricahua sector. I've sent all available biologists down to see if the wolves died from natural causes. We should get you an unmarked vehicle. Any chance you can spare time to drive to Silver City? I know you have a cabin there. If it's something you can manage, I'll swap out vehicles and get yours in for repair."

Wyatt had barely started and would hate to stop now. On the other hand, it might be better to take a few days now rather than after locating the Mission pack. "It's not my cabin so let me check with my friend who owns it. When I'm not there he sometimes lets other guests use it. Can I get back with you in a day or so?"

"Sure. Just take care. I'm damned tired of fighting ranchers over something they ought to be able to see rights the ecosystem. But telling you is like preaching to the choir. So you know, I'm having flyers printed up on the success of our program with the Fox Mountain pack. They've remained on their release range for five years. We have some testimonials from those area residents. I'll try to have a batch printed that you can take back for distribution."

"Sounds good, Joe. I'm for anything that helps people understand there's room on our planet for wild animals and domestic." He said goodbye and went back inside.

The cook signaled his pizzas were ready. Wyatt paid and carried the boxes out.

He soon left the town behind. He slowed when he approached a corner where he knew there was a cattle crossing. The ranch road to Spiritridge turned off the main road shortly after passing the crossing. It was a good thing he'd cut his speed. Not only was he staring directly into the sinking sun, but a large flock of sheep, not cattle, were moseying across the highway.

Because he heard dogs barking, Wyatt put his SUV in Park and opened his door, hoping to see the animals he'd caught sight of earlier. But the coloring wasn't right. The two dogs were sleek yellow Labs in the company of a young boy and a girl, who were probably the sheep owner's kids.

Wyatt settled back, refastened his seat belt and prepared to wait for the flock to pass. A bit tired of delay after delay, he drummed his fingers on the steering wheel and toyed with the idea of phoning Tandy to let her know he had the pizzas and was on his way.

At last the final woolies passed by. Dust began to clear and he saw the boy close the gate so no sheep could turn back. More than ready to roll again, Wyatt fired up his motor and drove to the ranch turnoff.

It so happened he drove in just as Tandy, Scotty and Manny were exiting the barn. He parked halfway between the main house and the casitas, figuring he could give the old cowboy his liniment and his pizza.

Then he'd be available to unload the heavy bag of dog food he'd bought for Tandy.

She jogged up to his door, leaving Manny hobbling along and Scotty skipping with his dog.

"Good grief," she yelped as Wyatt started to climb out. "What in the world happened to your car? Did it look like that yesterday? I remember passing it this morning and don't recall seeing all those awful marks."

Wyatt hadn't intended to bring the incident up. He didn't want to worry her—she might think someone would do the same to her since she was renting him a place to stay. "It happened in town. I didn't see the perpetrator. Sheriff Anderson had me fill out a complaint and he took photos. Can you take the pizzas? I'll give Manny his order then haul everything else into your house."

Tandy nodded, but her gaze remained on the damage until Scotty ran up and flung his arms around Wyatt's legs. "Did'ya remember to get us pizza, Wolf Man?" he asked. "I love, love, love pepperoni pizza."

"Scotty." Tandy tugged him away. "Mr...uh... Wyatt was about to give me the pizza boxes. I need you to open the house. I'll take these to the kitchen and bake them." She handed the boy the house key. "Go on. Scoot. And please don't call him Wolf Man."

"I sure hope the pizza cooks fast. Wait!" He spun back around. "Were you able to find a wolf book at the library? Sorry if you don't like me to call you Wolf Man."

Feeling a bit like he'd been hit by a semitruck, Wyatt let the boy's run-on chatter roll over him until

Manny arrived, took in the scene and laughed. "That boy can talk an ear off a flea. I'll take my order off your hands, Wyatt. Today was warmer. My joints feel some better. But I hope you found liniment. I can still use it."

Wyatt opened the back door to the SUV, ducked inside and found Manny's things. He passed them to the man and gave Tandy the two larger pizzas. He actually hoped she'd go on in. He'd like to ask Manny about the hybrids.

She drew Manny's attention to the scratched paint. "Any idea who might do something like this?" The man had worked for her parents from the time they'd bought the ranch. "You know everyone who lives around here. And probably most newcomers. People never used to even lock their houses or barns. I can't recall anyone ever having anything like this happen, can you?"

In the fading light, Manny bent closer and studied the marks. "Looks like you sideswiped a fence post or a telephone pole. What happened?"

"I don't know. I can only guess," he said, returning to slip out his book before lifting the remaining bags from the back seat. "I notified my boss. He's going to arrange for me to trade it for an unmarked vehicle. It's getting late. Shouldn't you both put your pizzas in to cook?"

As if Tandy got the message that he'd rather not discuss the incident, she tightened her hold on the pizza boxes and turned away.

He immediately felt bad. He certainly hadn't meant to dismiss her. He just thought it'd be worse to turn wolf dogs into a big deal. Especially because he didn't want Scotty to grab hold of it and start asking endless questions. "I was in the grocery store when it happened, Manny. Someone keyed my vehicle. It could've been personal, or a random act by hoodlums. Say it is personal, like aimed at driving me away from staying to do my job with the wolves. Maybe the less attention given the act, the better. What I don't want is to bring more anger down on Tandy and Scotty."

"I agree. Curtis would appreciate you caring about her and the boy. When she told me about how Preston Hicks ranted at the local rancher's meeting, I recommended she lay low and avoid that group. At my age, I can't help thwart any problems. I tried to help her hire a younger cowhand. Three times I thought we had someone, only to learn Preston Hicks or Jim Haskell swooped in and offered them higher wages. I'm gettin' stonewalled trying to buy her a bull, too. She ordered one from Stew Darnell. He keeps making up excuses about why he can't deliver."

Wyatt closed the back door to the SUV with his hip. "So you think it's deliberate? The not selling her a bull? Why wouldn't her money be as good as anyone else's?"

"Dunno. What if Pres Hicks warns Stew if he helps Tandy build her herd they'll freeze him out of the group that negotiates the best market prices come selling time? I don't know if that's a fact. I'm set to see Darnell tomorrow. If he weasels out again, I plan to ask him point-blank, why. See if he'll admit there's skulduggery afoot."

Shifting his load of grocery bags with the one from

the bookstore, Wyatt gazed at the clouds rolling in. "If Darnell agrees to sell Tandy a bull, great. If he dodges, I have a friend in New Mexico who sells a couple types. I have to drive up there to switch out my SUV. I'm sure Loki would give Tandy a good price."

The old fellow chuckled. "That'd fox 'em. Why don't you tell Tandy? I'm going in to bake my supper. I'll let you know what happens with Stew. If I get a bull I'll bring him home tomorrow. I want to see Tandy succeed in reviving the ranch to put down roots for her and Scotty. Curt would want that."

"Well, good luck with Darnell."

Manny inclined his head, turned and limped off just as Scotty called from the house, "Wolf Man... er...Wyatt. Mama wants to know if you're gonna come in for pizza? After we eat, can I have the library book?"

Wyatt hurried into the house. "I bought you a book that you can keep, Scotty. Help put groceries away for your mom, and after pizza, we'll look at it."

Tandy was so silent as he and Scotty bustled around the kitchen storing the milk, eggs and dog food, Wyatt was left with no doubt but that he needed to clear the air. After folding the sacks and setting them on the counter, he washed his hands at the kitchen sink. "Ah, you fixed a salad, too. Great. That makes pizza less of an unhealthy meal." He winked at Tandy and saw her eyes widen, and he noticed her lips twitch like she wanted to smile. Or rather like she didn't want to give him a smile.

Wyatt pulled out her chair, clearly surprising her. "Listen, I'm sorry for sounding as if I was doling out orders out there. I thought Manny would want to take his pizza home and get off his feet. Instead he decided to chat."

Tandy put a helping of salad on Scotty's plate. "I guess I'm touchier than I should be. A habit I developed in the service. New male recruits often overlooked the stripes denoting my rank. I'm not in the military now." She met his eyes and issued an apologetic shrug. "And you did us a favor by bringing supper and doing my shopping, which saves me a trip to town."

"And Mama, he bought me a book about wolves. He said it's mine to keep. That's so cool." Scotty bit into his first slice of pizza. "Oh, this is the yummiest supper we've had since we moved here."

Tandy and Wyatt exchanged silent mirth as they both tore off their slices.

Wyatt let a few moments pass before he spoke. "Manny mentioned you've been trying to hire a second cowboy but haven't found anyone available."

Tandy set down her pizza and wiped her hands on the paper towel next to her plate. "It seems other ranchers offer to pay them more. I can't raise my offer until after I see what my first cattle bring at market."

"I just wanted to say if you need an extra hand with anything while I'm here, my work hours checking on the wolf pack are flexible. I think Manny will tell you I did okay cowboying when your dad was so ill. Before college I helped on a buddy's family ranch."

"That's generous of you. I have a lot to learn about running a ranch. Manny should retire, but I'm so thankful he agreed to lend me a hand. I feel bad, though, because I know riding, roping and even walking sometimes hurts his old bones."

When she said "bones," the hound got up from under Scotty's chair and padded around to gaze up at Tandy with soulful eyes.

Scotty laughed. "Mr. Bones thought you were talking about him, Mama."

She gave the dog a piece of the ham from her pizza.

"Hey, I thought you said not to feed him at the table," Scotty accused.

"I did. That was a rare treat."

Scotty turned to Wyatt. "If you help Mama with the cows, can we help you hunt for wolves?"

"Uh...probably not. Today I didn't find them near easy walking paths. My next trek will be higher into the mountains. I'll have to be on the lookout for paw prints, or follow noise on my homing device from the wolves' collars. There may still be snow up there, too, so it'll be cold as well as tedious."

"Can you show me how you look for paw prints?" Scotty asked as he took another piece of pizza.

"I can show you how to recognize Mr. Bones's prints, and how they differ from a rabbit, a horse or other creatures that may hunt mice around your barn. Uh, if it's okay with your mom," he added.

"I'm fine with it as long as you don't follow them into the woods, Scotty. It's too easy to get turned around and lost in there."

"Definitely," Wyatt stressed. "I carry a GPS and I have a regular old-style compass if my electronics stop working."

"I'm full," Scotty said. "Can I see the wolf book now?"

"Maybe Wyatt hasn't finished eating," Tandy chided. "Wrap the rest of your pizza and stick it in the fridge to eat tomorrow."

"Yay. Pizza two times in a row." The boy hopped up and ran to get foil.

While he was rummaging in a drawer, Wyatt leaned toward Tandy. "As well as a book, I ran across a poster of a wolf family. I bought it, but if you think Scotty's too curious about wolves, I won't give it to him."

"Oh, he'll love it. His cousin in Hawaii had surfing posters on his wall. Scotty was always envious. He didn't have his own room at my sister-in-law's."

Wyatt ate the last of his salad and excused himself from the table. He retrieved the sack from the bookstore and unrolled the poster for Scotty and his mom to see.

"Wow, wow! I love it. Mama, can we hang it across from my bed so when I wake up I see it? Like where Mark tacked up his surfer dudes?" Not waiting for his mother to say yes or no, Scotty flung his arms around Wyatt. "My daddy never bought me nothing. He's not dead, Mama said. But he's gone. I won't see him anymore and I don't care. This is the best present I ever got. Can you stay here always, Wyatt? I know Mama said you're only here 'til you find the wolves. Why do you gotta go away?"

Seeing the shocked expression on Tandy's face, Wyatt unwound Scotty's arms. "I'm glad you like the poster. Let's sit and I'll read you part of the book."

The boy plopped down immediately, and Wyatt thought he'd smoothed over an awkward situation. At least he did until he noticed the pleat between Tandy's eyebrows as she jumped up and hurriedly began to clear the table. Wyatt wondered if he should have said more to extricate himself. Surely she didn't think he was trying to usurp the place of Scotty's father. He'd have to find a minute alone to assure her that wasn't so.

Chapter Three

Tandy suddenly felt angry all over again at Dan. She had bought Scotty birthday and Christmas gifts and marked them from her and Dan. How could their son be aware his father had never contributed anything? Had she accidentally sounded negative when explaining their divorce? She'd tried to be evenhanded. No matter how it hurt her, she hoped someday Dan would regret turning his back on his son.

While loading the dishwasher, she listened to Wyatt reading and explaining the pictures that went along with the story. There was no mistaking Scotty's delight. She had to smile over his rapid-fire questions. And yet the man kept up.

Soon done in the kitchen, Tandy still lingered. She didn't want to interrupt them so she assembled ingredients for chocolate chip cookies and got busy mixing. It didn't take long.

The timer sounded when the first sheet was done. Suddenly Scotty appeared beside her as she took the pan from the oven. He clutched the book and poster and literally bounced up and down with excitement, almost tripping over Mr. Bones.

"Mama, those smell so good. Can Wyatt and I have some? And will you take a picture on your phone of me with my book and poster? I wanna send it to Mark. Then can I call him? I bet he doesn't know mama and daddy wolves stay together their whole lives. And their pups go off like people kids do. Wyatt said if either the mama wolf or daddy die, they live with the pack but don't get married again. Did you know that?" He moved closer to the stove, turning serious when she eyed him with a slight frown. "Okay, wolves don't really get married 'cause they don't got churches like us, but it's com...com...what's that word you used, Wolf Man? Uh, Wyatt," he rushed to say, no doubt because Tandy set the pan of cookies down really hard.

"I said they have a committed relationship," Wyatt whispered to Tandy, walking into the kitchen. "I could've said studies suggest wolves mate for life, but then I'd have to explain what that means." He wrinkled his nose and scratched the side of his neck, all while offering Tandy a self-conscious shrug. "I was explaining how wolf packs resemble a town in how often families band together."

Finding his discomfort endearing, Tandy slanted him a smile. "Raising curious, precocious kids can be a challenge. Scotty, let me unload these cookies to the cooling rack and put the next pan in to bake before you take any."

As she worked, she eyed her son. With her having been away, she worried that he hadn't received many gifts for no reason. Thanks to Wyatt, right now

Scotty was dancing on air. It buoyed her spirits to see him so exuberant.

"I suppose you can call Mark. Let's see, it's still early enough in Honolulu so you won't interrupt their dinner." She checked her watch as she deftly set the timer again.

"I can take his picture if you'd like," Wyatt said. "I'll set up his call if you need to refill that pan. I'd hate for you to burn those great-smelling cookies."

"That would be helpful, thanks." She wedged her phone out of her pocket.

Wyatt reached for it and their hands tangled. Tandy almost dropped the phone. He caught it, and she mumbled, "Mark's number is under Lucinda, his mom's name."

Touching her arm briefly as he slipped by her, Wyatt glanced around the small kitchen. "How about you go back and sit on the couch, Scotty? You can unroll the poster, hold it to one side and have the book on your lap. That way we'll get everything in one photograph."

"Yay, yay, hurray! Mark will be so jealous. That's the right word, isn't it, Mama?" Stopping at the door, Scotty flung the question back over his shoulder. "That's what Mark used to say about me when he pinned up new surfing posters."

"You'd only use that word if you feel unhappy that someone else received a gift or got an award. Being jealous or envious doesn't reflect well on you. Or in this case, on your cousin. You boys should be pleased if good things happen to each other."

Watching Scotty pause to process that, Wyatt actually didn't expect him to understand. Yet it was evident when he did.

"I liked all of Mark's posters, Mama. I guess I shouldn't have wished some were mine." His worried features reassembled into a grin. "I want him to like my poster. But if he doesn't, it's okay. Mark didn't know any real surfers, but I know a wolf man. Come take my picture, Wyatt." He disappeared into the adjacent room.

Tandy's hands stilled above the last drop of dough she'd placed on the cookie sheet. Briefly her gaze collided with Wyatt's twinkling eyes. She took a deep breath and shook her head. He only offered a lopsided smile in return as he left the kitchen. He seemed to understand what she was trying to do.

Shortly she removed the next batch of cookies and loaded up another one, and spent a moment listening to the excitement in her son's voice as he talked to his older cousin. She placed several cookies on a plate then turned to take them into the living room as a carrot to entice Scotty to not talk forever. She ran right into Wyatt, who'd stepped back beneath the arch and stood watching her somberly. His hands flew to her waist to steady her.

"What is it? Are they not getting along?" The earlier twinkle had faded from his eyes and his jaw had a serious set.

He didn't let go of her. "A while ago when Scotty spoke about his father…well, I hope you don't think I overstepped my bounds. I know we'd discussed me getting him a book from the library. I should've asked your permission before I bought one instead. The poster was an impulse buy."

"It's okay," she rushed to say, stepping back until his hands dropped to his sides. "If anything I should've realized Scotty was affected by problems that blew up between Dan and me." She handed him the plate and stood rubbing her arms.

"Do you want to talk about it?"

"Well, we married in the haste that often comes when soldiers learn they're about to be sent off to fight. The long and short of it is I wanted children and had no idea Dan didn't until I learned I was pregnant. I thought he had a change of heart when conflicts erupted and we were both deployed. Wrong." She rubbed her arms harder.

Wyatt set the plate on the counter and took her hands. "It's okay. It's really none of my business."

She squeezed his hands then let go. "Anyway, due to deployments Dan and I saw little of each other. Maybe if we'd lived together he would've wanted children."

"What a stupid man. Scotty's a great kid."

She returned to loading dough on an empty cookie sheet. "It hurts to look back and see how often I made allowances for Dan when he didn't remember Scotty's birthday, or mine. I told myself he'd been promoted and had more on his plate than buying gifts. With that book and poster, you made Scotty happier than his father ever did. If I didn't share the blame for missing so much, I'd be giving you more credit."

"I don't need credit. I need a cookie." Wyatt

grinned crookedly. "It's been ages since I've had a homemade chocolate chip cookie."

"Heavens, eat a couple. I'll send some home with you, too." She gave him the plate.

"Is the coffee still hot? By the way, I never thanked you for stocking my kitchen with a pound of Hawaiian coffee. It's tasty."

"You're welcome. And help yourself. I didn't turn off the coffee maker." She gestured to the pot.

Wyatt moved behind her and poured his coffee as the oven bell blared.

She and Wyatt bumped hips again in the small kitchen. She felt how solid he was when she bent to drag out the steaming cookie tray and replaced it with one she'd just filled. Then her brain turned to mush for a moment because he hadn't moved and she brushed against him again while scooping fresh cookies onto the cooling rack.

Feeling klutzy, she said, "Why don't you take the plate in to tempt Scotty to get off the phone. Remind him not to share with Mr. Bones, though. In fact, let me get him a doggie treat. He begs so sweetly that both Scotty and I have difficulty denying him." She set down the pan, sucked in a deep breath and hurried to the pantry.

"Dogs, cats and kids learn early that certain beseeching tilt of their head."

"And their eyes," she added, handing him the doggie treat. "We service men and women carried gum and candy for kids we met in the poorest parts of war zones. We couldn't resist their big, hopeful eyes. I think eyes speak a universal language."

"Yours are striking. Some eyes aren't lively. Yours are," Wyatt said, juggling the plate, his mug and the dog jerky.

"Really?" Not in the habit of receiving compliments from men, Tandy was embarrassed. "I've never considered my eyes as anything but dull. I'll take lively as a compliment. As a kid I wanted blue eyes. Or brown eyes flecked with green or gold."

"They're not dull at all." Wyatt cleared his throat. "I hear Scotty jabbering away. I'd better go deliver these cookies and the doggie treat." He set down his mug, bit into one of the cookies and held her gaze a moment longer. "These are definitely as good as they smell," he said.

"Thanks." Tandy grabbed the oven mitts for something to do with her idle hands.

Wyatt shoved the rest of the cookie into his mouth, grabbed the plate and ducked back into the living room, leaving her combing through their last exchange. In doing so she found a few more reasons to give the man credit. In her old work environment some of her male counterparts griped endlessly about food in the mess halls. Certainly none would've ever been caught dead complimenting a fellow soldier's eyes, either. That placed Wyatt in a category by himself.

Suddenly at loose ends, Tandy thought she'd better be on guard against growing too fond of his compliments. The last thing she wanted was to fall for any man so soon after her hurtful split from Dan. As nice and as different as her renter and her dad's former friend seemed to be, it wouldn't do to be gullible.

While her heart was mending, she had Scotty's heart to consider. His earlier comment drove home how, as young as he was, his father's neglect had left a hole.

She'd gone back to filling the last cookie sheet when Scotty came running into the kitchen. He clutched the phone and was shoving a cookie into his mouth. "Mama, Mama," he said around the gooey confection, "will you take a picture of me and Wolf... uh, Wyatt?" The boy wiped his mouth with his arm, spreading chocolate across his cheek. "Mark doesn't believe I know anybody who helps wolves. He said I hafta prove it by sending a picture. He says you probably bought me the book and poster."

"Honey, you have cookie crumbs all over your face and I have uncooked dough all over my hands. Let your cousin think what he will. You know the truth."

"But he thinks I'm lyin' and I'm not." The boy's face crumpled.

"Oh, all right." Tandy huffed out a breath in exasperation. "Tell Mark you'll text him back. Wash your face while I wait to unload the last cookie sheet." She quickly checked over her shoulder and saw Wyatt standing under the arch again, still holding the plate of cookies.

Tandy grabbed for her son. "Scotty, wait. Did Wyatt agree to have his picture taken with you and sent to Mark? You can't shoot and ship off photos without the other person's consent."

Scotty showed his shock by how fast he stopped. "Is it all right?" he begged Wyatt. "You heard me tell Mark you aren't a werewolf. I told him my mom said those aren't even real. Doesn't matter that Mark has a movie where men go into the woods and change into wolves."

Wyatt laughed. After finding his mug and taking another swig, he said jovially, "I'm fine with a photo. I did wonder about it when I heard you telling your cousin I'm not a werewolf. You should just use my name, though."

"Yep." Scotty plopped the phone down on the kitchen counter and, after punching his fist in the air, disappeared down the hall.

Tandy let out a sigh. "I keep thanking you for things, but thank you for indulging him. I wasn't aware of the rivalry that apparently developed between him and Mark while I was deployed. He has two other cousins, both girls. I guess it's natural that he mostly hung out with Mark even though he's a few years older."

The oven bell went off and she spun around to rescue the cookies.

"You're still busy. Should we just do a selfie? Frankly I don't know why his cousin thinks seeing me proves I work with wolves, but I could tell listening to one side of the conversation that the other boy thought Scotty was making up a story. I suppose if they spent time practically as siblings that'd explain it."

Scotty exploded back into the room. His face was clean, but his hair in front stood on end where he'd obviously scrubbed off with a towel. Tandy's heart gave a little lurch when obviously seeing it, too, Wyatt casually brushed a hand over her son's spiky hair until it fell into place.

"Where's a good spot for a selfie?" he asked, picking up Tandy's phone from the counter.

"Maybe you should sit on the couch," Tandy said. "With cookie fixings all over in here, the background might look too messy."

Dashing over, Scotty hugged her. "The kitchen smells yummy. Too bad Mark can't smell it over the phone. How can talking and pictures go all the way to Hawaii, but cookie smells can't?"

Tandy rolled her eyes at Wyatt over the top of her son's head. "If you can explain that while you take your picture, I'll fill a Tupperware with cookies for you to take home."

His deep laugh filled the room. "Come on, Scotty. I'll tackle a simple version of quantum mechanics versus optics."

The two went into the living room and Tandy realized it'd been a long time since she felt this lighthearted. For that she might bake cookies more often.

She had the last pan out and a to-go container ready for Wyatt by the time her son skipped back into the kitchen. Scotty bubbled over with how easily they'd sent two pictures to Mark, who'd rung back to say he was sorry for doubting his cousin.

"I'm yawning, so Wyatt said we can finish reading the book tomorrow. Is that okay, Mama?"

Wyatt had entered the kitchen to return Tandy's phone to the counter. "We read the first chapter. It deals with tracking wolves. Tomorrow afternoon, if you don't mind, I said I can show Scotty how to see the difference between Mr. Bones's paw prints and other tracks, like a horse or cow. Then maybe read more of the story."

She nodded. "Here are the cookies I promised you. Thanks again for the pizza, the book and the poster, and for helping Scotty call Mark. Tomorrow will be a routine day of us checking cattle in the grazing area and moving another batch out of arroyos. I don't know if you'll have time to join us there. It might be too dark to see prints around the barn when we return." It dawned on Tandy that she was rambling. She nervously took a breath. "Anyway, Scotty and I will be on our own tomorrow. Manny plans to see Stewart Darnell about a bull and I assumed you'd go out to find your wolves." She briefly set a hand on Scotty's shoulder, then lifting it she moved toward the front door with Wyatt.

"That's my plan." He grabbed his jacket and hat and wagged the cookie container. "Thanks for these. The one I ate tasted exactly right to satisfy my sweet tooth." He opened the door and stepped out onto the porch.

Tandy started to go out to say goodbye but heard her phone ring in the kitchen. "Scotty, there's my phone. You tell Wyatt good-night for us, lock up, then scoot on in and get ready for bed while I find out who's calling."

The boy yelled, "Bye, Wyatt. I love my presents. I can't wait to look at animal tracks tomorrow. I hope you have time. Thanks again for everything."

Glad to hear her son's good manners, Tandy hurried back into the kitchen to scoop up the phone. She was a little out of breath when she swiped it to answer without checking to see who'd called.

"I see you didn't waste any time moving on. Here I thought you were so broken up over Dan."

"Lucinda?" Tandy recognized her former sister-in-law's voice. "What are you talking about? You knew we were moving to my dad's ranch in Arizona."

"I'm talking about moving on and moving in with a new man. Don't play coy. The one in the photo Scotty sent Mark. Is the dude an ex or were you two carrying on the whole time I looked after Scotty?"

"Geez, Lucinda. Calm down. He's a wildlife biologist working on a wolf project in the area. He's renting a cabin from me, and he rented from my dad last year. The man's been kind to Scotty, and Scotty wanted to share his new things with Mark. But since Dan plans to remarry ASAP, what would be the big deal if I met someone I cared to date?"

The woman on the other end of the call sputtered. "It's just you acted so upset with what Dan did. By the way, he already married Su Lin. They'll be here next week, so it's better if Scotty doesn't contact Mark as much. Dan's going to be based at Fort Shafter for at least six months. The newlyweds will live with me until they find an apartment."

The news shouldn't have stunned Tandy, but it did. It wasn't that she expected Dan to not marry this soon. But she assumed he'd remain in the Philippines.

She gathered her shock and worked to control her fury. "I'll handle Scotty. You see Mark doesn't call him. And isn't it a damned shame your brother's decision has to affect our innocent kids?" Her voice cracked so she rushed to end the call. "It's getting late here and it's Scotty's bedtime. And I'd like it if you kept your nose out of my business." She stabbed the disconnect button but wondered how the gaiety she'd felt moments ago could so rapidly and thoroughly dissipate.

More anger coursed through her. How dare Lucinda accept one standard for her brother and expect something entirely different of her? Tandy had done her best to brush off Lucinda's snide jabs. She'd established in her mind that she wasn't looking for involvement with another man. However, neither was she averse to having a handsome, rugged, nice guy like Wyatt Hunt living a stone's throw away. Especially someone who treated her son so well.

"Mom, I'm ready for bed. But will you help me hang my wolf poster first?" Scotty hollered.

"Coming," Tandy called. She pocketed her phone. Somehow it felt like that small act gave her a final separation from her unsettled past. And her sense of well-being returned.

Chapter Four

The sun struggled to come up through a layer of clouds when Wyatt took his backpack out to his vehicle for another hike up the mountain. He heard a clanking metal sound, looked around and saw Manny at the barn hitching a horse trailer to his pickup. Realizing the arthritic man was having trouble connecting the tongue to the hitch, he jogged over to help.

"Hey, Manny. Need a hand?"

"Seems so. Some days these old fingers won't work."

Leaning down, Wyatt quickly connected the hitch and gave the ball an extra twist to make sure it was tight. "Any time I'm around, you only have to ask and I'll help. I know you were planning to retire soon."

"I was. But Curt was a good friend to me, which is why when his daughter asked my advice on the best way to rebuild Spiritridge Ranch, I had to answer the call."

Wyatt pinched his bottom lip and nodded. "I can see you wanting to give her the benefit of your experience. Isn't working when it hurts going overboard?"

"It's plain mean how ranchers in the community are ganging up on her."

"So you plan on pitching in until she hires someone? I'm sure she appreciates it."

"To make this ranch work well for her and Scotty, she needs one seasoned cowboy. Each time I figured her ad brought a possibility, they ended up feeding her half-assed excuses for not taking the job. It ain't right, I tell you."

"I've felt guilty since she said they gave her grief at the association meeting for renting to me. But you're saying they were biased against her even before anyone knew I was coming back?"

"Yep."

"On one hand I'm relieved to hear it's not only my presence causing Tandy grief. On the other, I don't understand because her family ranched here for years. Do you think at the bottom of it, it's because Preston Hicks wants this ranch?"

"I wish I knew. He didn't try to buy the place until Curt got sick. He pushed harder after the newspaper ran a story saying Tandy was leaving the army to claim her inheritance. Hicks already owns the biggest ranch around. At his age, what does he need with more land? Millie Dawson ran cattle down in the valley for twenty years, so it can't be the old-timers don't cotton to the notion of a woman rancher." Manny frowned.

"If they did I'd wonder what century they're living in."

"One where some of those guys participated in range wars over land leases, water rights, fencing and a host of other dumb things."

"Shows my ignorance. I thought all of that was ancient history. But I almost forgot. I have a question. Do you know if anyone's seen hybrid wolf dogs running loose in the area? Maybe up along the rim?"

"Wolf dogs?" Manny stripped off his hat and scratched his head. "I've heard a lot of grousing over your wolves. Don't recall any talk of hybrids. Why?"

"On my first hike above the foothills, I glimpsed an animal or two with wolf characteristics. They were bigger than wolves in my team's Mission pack. They disappeared in underbrush. I lost their prints."

"No ranchers run cattle up there, Wyatt. Do you think your wolves made off with some ranch dogs? Is that adding to the neighbors' anger?"

"What I know is our four adult wolves haven't been free long enough to have mated with cow dogs the size those were. Plus, our females were pregnant by their mates when we turned them loose. It's something we make sure to do."

"Then I've no idea. Sorry."

"Since you're going after a bull, would you casually inquire if there's been any talk of hybrids?"

"Stew Darnell lives on the flats. I'll ask, providing he'll talk with me at all."

"I'd planned to trek out today to hunt my wolf pack, but I can go along with you as backup." Wyatt grimaced. "Unless my being there would make things worse."

"It might. Thanks, though. If you can spare the day I'd rather you ride with Tandy and Scotty. Yesterday we moved half her cattle to leased grassland. It borders Hicks's spring range. I caught the flash of sun off glass. It could've been binoculars, like he was watching us. I didn't tell Tandy 'cause by the time I dug out my field glasses, the flash was gone. Hicks doesn't much like me. Never has. He's acting weird. Just sayin'."

"I can spare the day. I told Scotty I'd show him how to distinguish different tracks. For the fun of identifying a cow print from a horse or elk, or his dog's print from a rabbit. He seemed excited, and it's something as a lonely kid I spent hours learning."

"He is lonely. And full of spunk. He's not old enough to be of any real help herding cattle. But he's a trooper to stick with us all day. It's nice of you to take an interest. Curt wished he could've spent more time with his only grandson. Even if he'd lived, that wouldn't have happened. I 'spect Tandy might've stayed in the army."

"Would she have after her divorce?"

Manny hiked a shoulder. "I dunno. I never married or had kids. I know cattle and horses. I don't know squat about women. Curt hired me when a lot of folks around didn't trust Mexicans. Didn't matter that I was born and raised in Texas. My papa died when I was sixteen. Mama and my older sister went back to Mexico. I quit school and worked cattle drives until South Texas ranchers decided I was too old at forty. I kept moving north and found Curt. He kept me on thirty years and I outlived him. When my time comes I'm gonna ask Tandy to see I get buried near her folks. They treated me like family. That's why I'll do all I can to help her and the boy."

Wyatt mulled over the old cowboy's words. He

reflected for a moment on his own life. He'd long thought his parents shouldn't have had children. Like Manny, he felt closer to his best friend's family than his own. "Tandy needs your experience, Manny, so don't go digging your grave just yet."

"All I can do is my best. Well, I gotta get going," Manny said. "It's slow traveling with an empty trailer. With or without buying a bull, I won't be back until dark. Oh, look, I see Tandy and Scotty coming out of the house."

Glancing around, Wyatt caught her smile and his heart tripped faster, which it shouldn't be doing. He was here temporarily, at best.

Scotty barreled past his mom, launching himself at Wyatt. "Can we look at animal tracks now? Maybe Mama will wait."

Manny hesitated after opening the door to his pickup. "I suggested Wyatt saddle up and join you on the range today," he said, addressing the pleading boy.

"Really? That'd be so cool. Will you? Will you, huh, Wyatt?" Scotty unwound his arms to stare up at the tall man.

"What's cool?" Tandy inquired once she'd strolled into their orbit.

Manny had climbed into the cab of his truck, but he had yet to close the door. "I thought you could use another hand shuttling stubborn heifers from the canyon to the mesa. I took the liberty of suggesting Wyatt go along. Scotty was just adding his two cents. Wish me luck with Darnell so that by tomorrow we'll have a nice range bull to start growing your herd." He waved goodbye, slammed his door and immediately started his rig with a loud rumble.

Wyatt deftly edged Scotty and Tandy a fair distance away from the arc of the trailer. Swiveling at the hip, he asked Tandy, "Where's Mr. Bones? Manny's lead-footing it out of here and he's kicking up mud."

"Mr. Bones is still a puppy in some ways. Yesterday he got underfoot. I decided to leave him in the house. Are you really okay with filling in for Manny today? It's not necessary to take you away from your work. Manny's such a worrywart. Who would've guessed that of an old bachelor cowboy?"

"I want Wyatt to go with us," Scotty burst out, again throwing his arms around Wyatt's legs.

"I don't know that he's so much of a worrywart. But he knows all there is to know about raising cattle. He probably believes two or three riders have an easier task of keeping cows moving in a straight line. It's totally your call."

"Mama!" Scotty implored her again.

"Sure." She bobbed her head. "I just don't want you to feel obligated."

"I don't."

"Okay. I'll go saddle our mounts then."

As a man, Wyatt's first inclination was to tell her he'd saddle the horses. Then he resettled his cowboy hat and took a moment to gauge her true reaction. There was something in the tilt of her chin. Was it that she didn't want to impose on him, or more that she didn't want him thinking her incapable? He didn't. But, not wanting her to think the latter, he jerked a thumb toward his casita. "Let me grab my lunch from the house and a day pack. At least from what you said last night you're planning to be out in the canyons all day, right?"

"Yes, based on how long it took us to round up half the herd yesterday. Come on to the barn, Scotty."

"Hooray, hooray!" The boy let loose of the man and excitedly galloped off.

His mom rolled her eyes and grabbed him by the jacket collar to steer him toward where the horses and his mule were stalled.

Chuckling to himself, Wyatt quickly hid his mirth and set about locking up his vehicle and retrieving his lunch and thermos from the house.

When he entered the barn, Tandy handed Wyatt the reins to a long-limbed buckskin. "This is Bandito," she said. "I hope he's not feisty. I haven't ridden him yet. Manny exercises him. He's a backup in case my mare or Manny's gelding pulls up lame."

"He looks familiar. Did he belong to your dad?"

Her eyes widened. "Why, yes. Manny said he couldn't bear to part with the horses after Dad died. Scotty's mule, Patch, is new."

"Someday I'll be big enough to ride a horse," the boy said, looking at Wyatt from atop his saddle. "I want to ride fast sometimes and Patch pokes along." He made a face.

"I had a pony as a kid. They're smaller than a horse but can be unpredictable. I think for riding the canyons around here, a sure-footed mule is just right," Wyatt said, and it made the boy beam. "I'll follow you guys," he added, swinging into his saddle.

SEVERAL TIMES THROUGHOUT the ride into the winding canyons where most of Tandy's stock had wintered, she darted glances back to where Wyatt rode, bombarded by Scotty's litany of questions. She wasn't checking to see how the man was holding up, but more because he looked so darned fine sitting tall in the saddle. As well, he continued to field her son's endless queries on a range of subjects without showing any sign of agitation.

Her mind strayed to what it might be like if he stuck around to cowboy. He could pass for one in looks. But when his deep voice reached her and she heard his enthusiasm in telling Scotty about the numbers and types of endangered wolves, it was plain he loved his job. The warmth that spread through her from merely watching him cooled marginally.

She was first to reach an outcrop above an arroyo where ten or so heifers grouped together. "There's one batch of cows we need to round up," she called, interrupting the other riders' discussion about how deer, elk and moose differed.

She thought it obvious, by their antlers. But an almost-six-year-old had no clue. And Wyatt explained in greater detail having to do with height, weight, location and other pertinent facts seeming to interest her son. Who would have guessed? Perhaps she needed to sign him up for public schooling. Scotty was so eager to learn and she'd begun thinking she shouldn't homeschool him like her mom did with her. She'd have to look into the school-registration process this summer.

"So do we gather this group up and move them to

your spring feeding ground?" Wyatt asked, leaning an arm on his saddle horn as he studied the milling animals below.

"That's what Manny had us do yesterday. It's about a twenty-minute ride from here to the grazing mesa. Collecting small pockets of cows along the route got monotonous. However, Manny said they'd stay together more easily, which was true."

Wyatt nodded. "Trust him to know best. Looking back, I believe when I helped round up your dad's entire herd to ship to market, we carved them into manageable clusters. Manny and I moved them from Curt's lease to where we met the cattle trucks."

"That's right—you helped with the ranch chores last year. I guess you learned quite a bit."

"Yep. Really, though, because my parents did fieldwork at remote archaeological digs, I spent a lot of time with a ranch family in New Mexico. I grew up mucking barns, feeding and moving cattle."

Tandy sat straighter. "Then why didn't you become a rancher? How did you settle on the field you're in now?"

"My mother insisted I go to college. While there I took exploratory classes and gravitated toward biology, zoology, chemistry, conservation and animal husbandry. I think my mom's still disappointed I didn't elect to follow in her and Dad's footsteps as archaeologists. Why did you leave Spiritridge and choose to go into the army?"

"Yeah, Mama," Scotty said, moving his mule closer to her.

"When I was in junior high, TV news was filled

with stories about people in other countries being forced into a lifestyle they didn't want. Women and girls weren't allowed to attend school. Shortly after I entered high school we hosted army and navy recruiters. When the captain explained what the army did, it resonated with me."

"You sound nostalgic."

"What's nos…nos…?" Scotty asked, edging closer to Wyatt.

Maintaining his role as explainer, Wyatt addressed the boy. "*Nostalgia* sort of means missing something. I wondered if your mom's missing the army."

Tandy broke in. "Perhaps what you heard in my voice was more surprise to find I don't regret leaving it." Her gaze shifted to her son. "Scotty said he misses living in Hawaii."

"Not anymore," he was quick to toss out. "I did before you came to live with us," he said, beaming at Wyatt.

"Scotty!" His mother shook her finger at him. "Wyatt is renting one of our cabins."

"Well, it's the same thing," Scotty growled defensively. "I don't want you to go back to the army. Mark said Daddy and the person he married are gonna live with them. Daddy used to yell at me about everything. He never 'splained nothing."

Tandy's breath caught in her throat, and for a moment she felt heat climb her cheeks and was at a loss as to what to say. Finally she settled on correcting Scotty's grammar. "The proper word is *explained*, and you can't use it with *nothing*. It's *anything*. He never explained anything."

"That's what I said." The boy huffed indignantly.

Wyatt interrupted. "Enough said. Time's wasting. Let's ride down and get these heifers moving. Scotty, I assume Manny told you to make sure you always stay behind the herd. At least he told me a dozen times to not let cows surround me."

"Yep. He said that to us, didn't he, Mama?"

"That he did." Touching her heels to Butterscotch, she headed the mare into the arroyo, and the others followed.

The next half hour was consumed with getting hardheaded heifers to leave the spot they'd staked out in the narrow canyon.

Wyatt waved his hat and yelled, "Hi yi yi," several times at recalcitrant strays, making Tandy smile into her shoulder because he looked and sounded so much like a real cowboy. And soon Scotty imitated him. Seeing how happy he appeared had warmth blossoming in her chest. While it saddened her to learn this late that his dad had yelled at him, she took heart realizing he was young enough for the gentle kindness of others to erase those bad memories.

"Which way now?" Wyatt hollered to her once they'd cleared the canyon.

"Straight ahead. See how there's sort of a path cut through the mesquite and creosote bushes? Follow that."

He dug his cell phone out of his pocket. "Okay. I have the coordinates. I've got a compass app on my phone. I can't tell you how helpful it's been on a couple of my projects. Doesn't work out of satellite range." He stabbed a finger off in the direction of the mountain peaks.

"I should get that on my phone," she said, riding close enough to him she could see his phone screen. "I wonder if the army uses that feature."

"I have a hard time picturing you weighed down in soldier's gear. Not that I question your ability to command or shoot," he hastened to say.

"What do you mean then?" she asked sharply.

"You're uh, slender and feminine and pretty. Ah, I'd better quit before I insult you when I don't mean to at all."

Made self-conscious by his compliments, Tandy made a big point of starting to shoo the cows forward again.

Because much of the next section of terrain required them to string out in single file, Tandy and Wyatt both looked out for Scotty as they drove the herd to the lease.

"I remember this place now," Wyatt said. "It's where we rounded up your dad's cattle for market. Manny said he and Curt set the posts and fenced this entire grassland all by themselves. Should I go open the gate, or would that be stepping on your toes as ranch owner?" he added with a sly grin.

"Feel free." Tandy stood up in her stirrups and gazed over the backs of the animals stopped by the deer fence made of wire netting strung between rough-cut wooden posts.

Wyatt was off his horse and had the gate that swung inward almost open when Tandy called, "Wait!"

The heifers, most likely seeing grass and smelling water from the stream that bisected the property, tried to surge ahead past Wyatt.

"Why wait? I can't hold them back, Tandy," he said loudly, secreting himself and his mount behind the half-open gate.

"Where are the cows we brought here yesterday?" She fumbled in her saddlebag and pulled out field glasses. "Oh, no. Wyatt, they've broken down the fence on the other side of the creek. My cows are all mixed in with some belonging to Preston Hicks."

Her cracking voice spelled out her fear.

"Don't panic," Wyatt said calmly. "I'm sure this has probably happened before. At least it can happen with fencing this old. You and Scotty let these cows in while I ride over and see if it's something we can easily repair."

"Okay. I'll try to keep the current cows from crossing the stream. Maybe they'll be content chewing grass on this side of Cedar Creek."

Tossing her a thumbs-up, Wyatt mounted up and followed cattle tracks to the low spot where it was plain the previous occupants had crossed the water. Intent on finding the place where the fence went down, he located it and was concerned by what he saw. About to signal for Tandy to come look, he heard a cough. Raising his head, the last thing he expected to see was a large man astride a larger horse facing him with a rifle pointed at his chest.

"Whoa!" Wyatt spoke to Bandito and to the man holding the gun. He recognized Preston Hicks at the same moment it was evident the other man recognized him.

"Well, well. What in hell are you doing on my land, Hunt?"

"I'm not on your land. Yet. But I'm about to cross over to round up Tandy's cattle and drive them back here."

"Not so fast." Hicks sheathed the rifle, which at least left Wyatt less antsy.

"I'd think you'd be glad to not have her cattle eating your grass," Wyatt said.

"I'm taking a count. She's gonna owe me a substantial sum for putting her cows in with my registered bull. She may think trampling our joint fence is clever, but technically I could lay claim to a lot of her calves come fall. I'll settle for the standard covering fee of a hundred bucks per head. Roughly the little lady owes me about twenty-five hundred smackeroos."

"You're saying she did this so her cows could mix with your bull?"

"That's what I'm saying. She doesn't have a bull because no one in the area will sell her one." Hicks's mouth twisted in a sneer.

"You're wrong. That's where Manny is today, off buying a bull."

The rancher's face fell. Then he puffed up his chest just as Tandy rode up. "That's not gonna happen. No one in the ranchers association will help her." His glittering gaze shifted to Tandy and on to Scotty, who brought up the rear.

"What's going on?" she asked, glancing from Wyatt to her neighbor.

Butting in, Preston reiterated what he'd told Wyatt about paying for his bull's services.

Tandy gasped. "This is an accident. It must've happened after Manny and I left the last batch of my cows here yesterday afternoon then went on home. The fence was fine at five thirty."

"So you say." Hicks swept an arm around to encompass her cows surrounding his giant Hereford bull. "Yet your cows are in my pasture."

Wyatt strategically edged his horse between Tandy and Hicks. "What I see is that this wire fencing was cut, not trampled. I suggest we call Sheriff Anderson and have him or a deputy come take a look. I know the mesh is thin, but he can probably get fingerprints." As he said it, Wyatt watched for Preston's reaction, and was more than satisfied with the tight clenching of the other man's square jaw.

"You don't know what you're talking about," Hicks spat. "You're no rancher. Why don't you round up your wolves and take 'em and get the hell out of this area?"

Scotty barged his mule up next to Wyatt. "That's the bad man that yelled at Mama in the meeting. He can't make you go away, can he?"

"Scotty, hush." Tandy slid off her mare and walked over to inspect the fence. "I agree it's been cut, and I know my prints aren't on it." Staring at her neighbor, she untucked her phone, tapped a few keys and requested the number for the local sheriff.

"Hold up a danged minute," Hicks blustered. "Why

drag Doug Anderson all the way out here? The wire don't look sliced to me, but I'm willing to give you a freebie with these cows. I know Manny's coming back empty-handed, and you're gonna need old Hector once you come to your senses. Unless, of course, you sell the ranch, heifers and all to me." He moved his horse nose-to-nose with Tandy's. "For the sake of your dad, I'd give you a fair market price."

Her eyes cut to Wyatt, who shrugged.

"Why are you checking with him?" Hicks asked. "You're the sole owner of Spiritridge, right?"

"I am." Tandy drew herself up. "And I'm not selling. I suggest we round up my cows and bring them back where they belong. I trust you'll help us repair the fence."

"I gotta bad back, missy."

Wyatt spoke up. "I'll handle repairs so we'll know it's done right. I could use one new post and a couple dozen or so wire brads, though." He turned to Tandy. "If he can't provide those we can still phone Sheriff Anderson and ask him to swing past the hardware store on his way out to have a look-see. Whatever fool did this dropped his wire cutters." He pointed to where, indeed, the metal instrument peeked out from the base of a fence post.

That's when, from the way the older rancher's jaw dropped, Wyatt knew they had him dead to rights.

"Come up to the barn with me," he said, glaring at Wyatt. "Let Tandy and the kid drive her heifers back into her pasture. Boy," he added, scowling at Scotty, "keep away from old Hector. He's not always congenial."

"Mama, what does that mean?"

"It means you stay on this side of the fence."

Preston Hicks swung his big roan horse around and urged him up the hill.

Wyatt didn't like leaving Tandy and Scotty working in the proximity of that humongous bull. And he wasn't sure he wanted to follow Hicks. There was still the matter of his rifle. "I should be back in fifteen," he told Tandy. "If not, use a sandwich bag and pick up those wire cutters. Get them to Doug Anderson, downed fence be hanged."

"Surely you don't think he'll prevent you from coming back? I know he's curmudgeonly, but he's a church deacon and president of the Cattle and Sheep Ranchers Association."

Obviously she hadn't seen the gun. "Ask yourself who else would've cut this fence on purpose." He tapped Bandito's flanks with his boot heels, not wanting Hicks to get too far ahead of him. He got a few yards away and wasn't prepared when all at once the other man wheeled his horse around and galloped back.

"I don't like the idea of leaving a woman and boy around a sometimes randy old bull. It'd be best if you stay and help Ms. Graham round up her cows. I'll go home and drive my pickup back with everything you'll need to fix the fence. I'll toss in a new roll of wire mesh."

"What's the price for all of that?"

"Man, but you're suspicious. Can't an old friend of the gal's pa be neighborly?"

Wyatt knew that wasn't Hicks's nature. He must

be missing something, but at the moment he had no idea what. Since Wyatt also wasn't comfortable leaving Tandy and Scotty, he acquiesced. Turning back, he could say it was mostly Scotty who worried him. The boy was a bundle of energy. Expecting him to stay put was futile.

"Why are you coming back?" Tandy called. "Did he refuse assistance after all?"

"No. In fact, he expressed concern for you and Scotty. Clearly he has concerns about Hector's disposition."

"Me, too." She laughed awkwardly. "I feel as if he's eyeing me if not for his next meal, at least as an appetizer."

"Maybe he's really a big old teddy bear," Wyatt said.

"Wyatt, can I help gather cows?" Scotty navigated his mule through a few grazing heifers, which was exactly what Wyatt had feared.

"Sure. You take those closest to the fence and let me and your mom bring the ones farther away."

Looking gleeful, the boy got behind the nearest cow and slapped it on the rump with his hat.

"You've made him happy," Tandy said. "I would've been yelling at him to stay put. How is it you know so much about handling kids?"

Wyatt grinned. "I was one. Granted it was a long time ago. But some things you don't forget. Let's get started. I'd just as soon have all of your stock on your land by the time Preston returns."

"Do you really think he cut the wire?"

"I do." Wyatt circled behind a group of three heifers and he treated them to the same tactics that Scotty employed.

Tandy brought four into her pasture, and several more fell in line and followed their obvious group. "Why would he do that?" she asked, pulling abreast of Wyatt.

"He's determined to hassle you." Wyatt trotted his horse across the fence line again and collected another batch of heifers. When he and Tandy passed again, he paused momentarily. "If I thought it was all because you're renting to me, I'd move out tonight. I'm beginning to think he really wants your ranch."

"I've no idea why. He's not getting any younger and he already runs more cattle and sells more at market than any rancher around. I can't fathom why he dislikes me."

"Before you joined us he reiterated that no one is going to sell you a bull. He said to expect Manny to come home empty-handed. Blocking you from purchasing a necessity goes beyond pettiness. But, I have a friend who I'm sure will sell you a bull, Tandy. He lives in New Mexico."

"Hmm, thanks. It's something to consider. Here Preston comes in his pickup. Do you think we can move the last dozen cows before he gets all the way here?"

"Yes." Wyatt circled around the bull and let out a rebel yell. The remaining heifers left where they'd been grazing. Between Tandy waving her hat and Scotty stationed off to the left side, Wyatt scrammed the remainder of the herd well onto Tandy's lease.

Swinging out of his saddle, Wyatt handed her his

reins. "I've put up plenty of animal enclosures. Why don't you and Scotty patrol along the creek?" He swept a hand at the babbling water. "I'll string wire. Then before we go after another group of cows, why don't we settle down and eat lunch?"

"Ah. You're suggesting that to see if Preston hangs around and pulls any shenanigans."

Giving the toe of her boot a little squeeze, he smiled. "We think alike."

Hurrying over to Hicks's pickup, Wyatt let down the tailgate and quickly unloaded the items. "I can take it alone from here," he said. "You probably have other things needing your time."

"I'll just wait. You'll be using my hammer and posthole digger. Even though I have a bad back, I can steady the wire as you unroll it."

Because it was true he needed the other man's equipment, instead of responding, Wyatt shed his jacket and set to work. Since only one section was damaged and one post was down, he finished quickly.

Hicks put the hammer in his toolbox. "Do you mind lifting the posthole digger into the pickup bed? One of my cowhands rode in for lunch. He lifted it into the truck."

"No problem. You did the decent thing. Tandy only wants to make a home here for herself and her son."

The older man shot Wyatt a sour look. Without a word he strode to the pickup cab and climbed in. Only after he rumbled off did it strike Wyatt that Hicks hadn't moved like someone with a bad back.

Tandy walked up, holding the reins of both their

horses. "You seem perplexed. Did you two have words?"

He shook his head. "I feel his offer of help was phony."

"Maybe you're seeking reasons because he opposes your project."

"Maybe. Should we eat? I worked up an appetite. Hey, Scotty, are you hungry?" he called.

"Yeah. Mama packed me two slices of our leftover pizza. Yum." The boy slid off his mule and watched his mother open her saddlebags and pull out their lunch sacks.

Tandy handed Scotty one sack and retied her saddlebag.

"Mama, did you bag that cutter thing Wyatt said to take?"

She spun quickly and stared at Wyatt. "I didn't. We can do it after we eat. We'll have plenty of plastic bags left to scoop it up with."

"But it's not there anymore," Scotty declared, pointing to where the wire cutters had been.

Tandy and Wyatt shared a look of dismay. Then both frowned.

"Okay, there's why Preston offered to help and why he stuck around," Tandy said.

"I should have shot pictures. We have no way to charge him with mischief. In fact, the opposite. He can say we're lying. And by giving you wire and a post, he has proof he helped you." Wyatt's frown deepened.

"I told you he's a bad man," Scotty announced, plopping down on a stump. He opened his sack and wasted no time chowing down on the first of his two pizza slices.

Wyatt and Tandy sat side by side on a log. Their thighs occasionally rubbed against one another, and their arms, too. Neither pulled away. Halfway through lunch, Tandy admitted to herself that it felt good knowing this man had her back. Perhaps it was more.

Chapter Five

They'd made it back to the barn after transferring all remaining stock before a weak winter sun slipped behind a western peak. As expected, Scotty had the most energy left. When they finished unsaddling and feeding their horses and the mule, he begged Wyatt to show him how to find animal tracks.

"Scotty, maybe Wyatt's too tired. We all did a lot of work today, but he expended the most effort rebuilding that fence."

Wyatt squeezed her shoulder. "I'm fine. And there's enough light to check out some tracks around the corral. Unless you want him to call it a day."

"No." She sent him a grateful smile. "I don't want him to become a pest."

"I'm not a pest." Scotty sounded indignant.

"You're not," Wyatt assured. "Let's go over between the barn and the corral before we run out of daylight."

"I have stew in the slow cooker," Tandy said. "I'll go make biscuits to go with it. Oh, I hear Mr. Bones howling his head off. Is it okay if I let him out to join you?"

"Dog tracks will be a perfect contrast with those of rabbits, raccoons or other small animals that have likely trekked through the ranch."

Tossing him a smile, Tandy went off to the house and freed the dog, who'd been cooped up all day.

Wyatt gave Scotty a few minutes to play with his pet. Then, again reminding the boy they were losing daylight, he motioned past the corral. There, he'd observed a highway for small creatures making their way from spilled grain at the barn into the woods.

Kneeling, he pointed to clear tracks in the damp earth. "These are from a rabbit. See how many you can find. When tracking any animal you don't need every single print. Once you pick up two or three, walk in the general direction they're going and you'll see more."

"I see them." Scotty scampered along. "Mr. Bones's footprints are way different."

"That's right."

"I think there were two rabbits."

"Very good." The boy was more focused and learned quicker to see the difference in tracks than Wyatt imagined a kid his age could.

"Darn, it's too dark," Scotty said, getting up from the dirt and wiping off his knees.

"You did great for your first time. If I have time tonight I'll draw pictures of various animal tracks you can study. Then when you're out with your mom and Manny, you can be on the lookout and see how many different prints you can identify."

"Cool." Scotty called his dog back from the edge of the woods.

Tandy hollered at them to come to the house as Manny drove in.

"C'mon, Scotty. Let's go check out that bull."

"Goody. I hope he's bigger and meaner than the one the bad man owns." The boy took off running with Mr. Bones at his heels.

By the time Wyatt reached where Manny parked, Tandy had joined Scotty and they were peering into what looked to Wyatt like an empty stock trailer. In the light from the porch he saw the elderly ranch hand shaking his head even as he exited the cab and approached Tandy.

"So Stew didn't have a bull available?" She gripped Scotty's shoulders to keep him still.

"He had two, but he said both were sold and waiting to be picked up."

Tandy's face fell. "Do you believe him?"

"It's hard to dispute." Manny wore an unhappy expression, but he glanced at Wyatt. "You mentioned a friend who sells bulls. It may be the best option since I don't know of anyone else here."

Wyatt looked at Tandy. "You want me to check with Loki?"

At her nod, he dug out his cell phone, swiped a number and they all waited until he said, "Hey, Loki, it's Wyatt. Do you have any bulls to sell?"

"I have two. A Brangus and a Charolais. Why do you want a bull? I thought you were in Arizona chasing your wolves."

"He has two bulls." Grinning, Wyatt shot the others a thumbs-up then spoke into the phone again. "I have to swap out my SUV, and a friend is in the market for a bull. Is the cabin vacant in the next day or so? If it is, maybe I'll bring her and her boy to take a look at what you've got."

"The cabin's open. So, this rancher friend is a woman? Is there something Abby and I should know, you sly dog?"

"Loki, it's the woman I'm renting from, okay? I'll call you back if we work out travel plans. So long."

"You heard?" he asked at large after ending his call.

"I can't go off to New Mexico and leave the animals," Tandy exclaimed.

"Why not?" Manny asked. "If you moved the rest of the herd to grass along the stream, I'll keep an eye on them and the horses until you get back. What do you figure it'll take? Three or four days?" he queried, pinning Wyatt down.

"Five at most. My boss said he has a king cab pickup for me. We can truck the stock trailer up there. If the replacement for my SUV doesn't have a hitch, Loki and I can install one," he informed Tandy. "Think about it and let me know."

"Does he have kids?" Scotty asked.

"Yes, as a matter of fact. A son who's almost seven, and boy-and-girl twins who are four. He and I have been best friends since elementary school," he added.

"Manny, come in for stew and biscuits. It's all ready. We can talk more about this. Maybe you can go with Wyatt." Tandy turned toward the house.

"I have appointments with my dentist and orthopedic doctor in the next few days. You know how hard they are to schedule. You all go eat and talk it over.

I brought a hamburger from town. But remember, if you don't get a bull soon there'll be no calves come November." Plainly done with the conversation, he climbed into the pickup and drove toward the barn.

"We should go with Wyatt, Mama." Scotty skipped up the porch steps, Mr. Bones racing alongside.

"I guess we can. Manny's right about this year being wasted without a bull. I'll be darned if I'll pay Preston Hicks for the use of his."

"If we're up and out of here at daybreak, weather permitting we can cut travel time to a day each way with a full day up there."

After ushering everyone inside and to the kitchen, Tandy set out food while the others washed up. "I hate barging in on your friends," she said as they all took the same seats they'd had the previous evening.

"Loki and his wife come from big Apache families. Their ranch isn't on the reservation, but Abby has a huge family that often drops by. Loki has aunts, uncles and cousins galore who visit, too. They're used to people popping in. I stay there whenever I get time off. I'm sure you'll like them."

"I don't doubt that. If they're used to drop-ins, it'll be fine. I'm anxious to buy a bull, so again, thank you."

"You don't have to keep thanking me. Friends help friends. I'll be glad for company on an otherwise boring drive."

"Can we take Mr. Bones?" Scotty indicated his pet eating at his bowl.

Tandy paused, her spoon halfway to her mouth. "Heavens, he's too active to leave with Manny."

"Let's take him," Wyatt declared after swallowing a bite. "Loki has three or four dogs." Thinking about his friend's cow dogs made Wyatt remember he'd asked Manny to inquire at Darnell's if Stew knew of any hybrids in the area. Although, he was beginning to wonder if he'd seen things. He hadn't run across any tracks up the mountain or in the lower mesa today. Really, though, he couldn't think of another animal with that same profile.

"Wyatt, you said you'd read me more of the wolf book tonight. And you said you'd draw me pictures of animal tracks." Scotty, who'd been eating while the adults talked, scarfed down the last of his biscuit.

"If we have to leave at dawn," his mom said, "it has to be early to bed, young man. We can take the book. I'll read some to you on the drive. I guess I don't know about drawing animal tracks." She angled a glance between Scotty and Wyatt.

Wyatt blotted his lips with the paper towel by his soup bowl. "I'm going to the Game and Fish office, and they keep stacks of educational materials used at schools. I'll pick up a set that includes animal tracks. Some are pictures, others have written information your mom or I can read to you, Scotty."

"Goody. Since I have to get up way early, maybe I'll go to bed now." Darting around the table, he hugged his mom and then did the same to Wyatt. Calling Mr. Bones, the boy ran off down the hall.

Smiling, Tandy dipped her spoon back into her stew. "This is a first, him wanting to go to bed early. Early to bed, early to rise hasn't been his mantra."

"It was never mine, either. He reminds me of myself as a kid, except he's sharper. I showed him one set of rabbit tracks and he knew when that bunny joined a second one. He also reminded us about the wire cutters. Stuff sticks in his mind."

"That's music to a mother's ears. I was away from him so much. Now hearing some of the things he says, I fear he got shortchanged in the parent department."

"Not so." Wyatt stood and stacked his dishes. Reaching across Tandy, he picked up those Scotty had left. All at once he hesitated. Bent as he was, his face was close to hers. "Your hair smells good. Like apples." He leaned nearer.

She straightened, which put her even closer. "Uh, my shampoo is apple based."

"I like it, but I didn't mean to embarrass you." He hurriedly collected the dishes and strode to the sink.

"I'm not embarrassed. Actually, it's nice. Soldiers don't get compliments like that."

Finished rinsing dishes, he stacked them in the dishwasher. Turning, he saw her fiddling with her spoon but gazing at him with a yearning look that set his pulse racing. Caught up in an urge to kiss her, he said instead, "Then it's good you're a cowgirl now." He motioned to the door. "I forgot to ask Manny something. I'll go do that and see you in the morning."

"I forgot to tell him about the fence. Will you fill him in? Do you realize how lucky I was you were along today? At Manny's age, could he have repaired that fence?"

"He was fixing fences before you or I were born," Wyatt said lightly.

"You're right. His arthritis bothers him more than I like. I need to hire someone to replace him, but maybe I'll have to look farther afield to find a new cowboy. When we get back I'm going to attend the next cattle and sheep owners meeting and tell them point-blank what I think of their crummy tactics."

"Maybe that's what they need. To be publicly shamed," Wyatt said.

"Providing they even let me in the door." Tandy trailed him out so she could lock up behind him.

Wyatt had no idea why, but instead of just leaving, he stopped and hugged her. "Spiritridge Ranch is your birthright. They're bound to respect you more if you stand your ground." He withdrew quickly and struck out for Manny's casita without looking back. He guessed his hug shocked her, too, because he didn't hear her shut the door until he was halfway to Manny's.

He wondered if she'd mention it in the morning. And what would be his response? He couldn't fall for her. That wouldn't be good for either of them. While it was plain they were both lonely, his job here would soon be over.

But shoot, he'd gotten ahead of himself, he mused, stopping to rap on Manny's door. All he had to give him the notion Tandy might be interested in him were a couple of affectionate glances and invitations to a home-cooked meal or two.

Wyatt heard Manny shuffling to the door. "Your light was on, so I figured you hadn't turned in yet," he said after the door opened a crack.

"I fell asleep in front of the TV. Did you talk Tandy into going after a bull?"

"Yes, but I wondered if you'd asked Darnell about hybrids?"

"He said he doubted any rancher would own a hybrid. My feeling is he's reluctantly going along with the rest of the association about the bulls."

"Well, Tandy may confront the lot of them at the next meeting. Oh, hey, another thing we neglected to tell you…she had a section of fence down today." He launched into relaying all that had gone on with Preston Hicks.

"What's wrong with that man? He's always been the big cheese in the area, but he didn't used to be mean."

"You've been here a long time. I thought maybe you'd know why he's picking on Tandy."

"He's always been a leader." Manny pulled a wry face. "It's like he's gone tetched in the head."

"I suppose that's a possibility. He never made any secret of not liking me, and he's the most vocal about ridding the earth of wolf predators. He wouldn't listen to my team's ideas on how to help cattle and sheep ranchers coexist with wolves."

"Ya got that right."

"How much do you think my job is to blame for his antagonism toward Tandy? I'm prepared to pitch a tent in the forest."

"Dunno. I do know he badgered her to sell before he had any idea you'd show up and rent from her. I hope you stick around. I'm not able to stand up against him like I could've done even half a dozen years ago."

"As long as I'm here I'll watch her back. When I can, that is. There will be days I'm off and gone doing my work with the wolves. And once my mission here is done, I'll be sent elsewhere."

"That's too bad. I'd hoped you two…never mind. She needs a young guy with a strong back around. And you've won over her boy and his dog."

Something about hearing it stated so bluntly troubled Wyatt. Tandy and Scotty deserved a permanent champion in their lives. It didn't seem as if they'd had that in Scotty's dad. "I won't keep you longer," he said, shoving his hands in his pockets. "We agreed to leave at dawn. You have our phone numbers if need be. My hope is to hold the trip to three days. One of us will let you know if it takes longer."

"Don't rush back on my account. You'll likely hit snow going over the rim. Driving back with the weight of a bull will be slower out of necessity."

"Gotcha." Wyatt bounded off the porch and noticed Tandy's house was dark. He still needed to toss a few clothes in a duffel and set his alarm. Besides packing, he needed to text Loki to expect them tomorrow evening.

He had a long day's drive ahead and it'd do no good to stay awake wrestling with concerns for Tandy and feelings he couldn't develop for her.

THE MORNING EASTERN sky was barely pink when Tandy, a sleepy Scotty and his wide-awake dog beat Wyatt out to his SUV.

"Hey," he said, emerging from his casita. "I had

to wait for coffee to brew so I could fill a thermos. Hope I haven't kept you waiting long."

"We just got here. I brought coffee, too," she said, lifting a thermos bag.

Scotty yawned. "She made me hot chocolate, but can Mr. Bones and me sleep longer on the drive?"

Chuckling, Wyatt tweaked Scotty's cowlick. "Sure. Your mom can sit up front with me and give you and the pup the whole back seat." He opened the hatch and stored their bags. "I see you packed light. I didn't know what to expect so I unloaded all of my equipment last night."

"It's army training." Tandy opened the back door and boosted Scotty and the dog in. "Here's your pillow and blanket, but be sure you buckle up."

"Cool, I get to use a big-people seat belt instead of my booster."

"I didn't realize he needed a kid seat," Wyatt said, slamming the hatch. "Let's unhook yours and install it in my vehicle for the trip."

"I hate to put you out. He's big for his age. But, when I got my Arizona license he was with me. The lady at the DMV said the new kid seat belt law was strict."

"It's no problem. Hop in, we'll drive over to where you're parked."

"Aww, Mom."

"It's better to be safe than sorry," Wyatt told the boy. "Manny reminded me last night that we could hit snow in the mountain pass."

"Snow," said the sleepy voice from the back seat. "I've never seen snow, 'cept on TV or Mark's DVDs."

"Really?" Wyatt stopped next to Tandy's vehicle.

"He was born in Hawaii and lived there until our move. Santa even arrives by surfboard there."

"I've only seen *that* on TV," Wyatt said, laughing again. It didn't take him long to remove and reset the booster. Minutes later Scotty was buckled up with his pillow and blanket.

Manny came out of his cabin dressed for work and waved them off as daylight shone in a thin strip of lavender and gold between mountain peaks and a layer of clouds.

"I hope I'm doing the right thing," Tandy murmured as she poured coffee into her travel mug.

"I hate to call your neighbors enemies, but showing them you won't be cowed by their silly pact to hold you back is good, don't you think?"

"Yes." She settled back, clutching her mug as they made their way down the highway. "I wish things were different. I wish we could become part of the community like my parents were. It's what I imagined when we moved here."

"My grandmother always said stop wishing life away and start living it."

"Smart lady. With luck, if we don't budge, maybe eventually neighbors will accept us."

"Exactly." Wyatt braked as three elk crossed the road.

Tandy hurriedly reached back and kept Mr. Bones from sliding off the seat. "I forgot how many deer and elk live around here. I'm surprised I haven't encountered any when tending my cattle."

"We've climbed around six hundred feet from

where your ranch sits, and you run cattle several hundred feet below that. In the last five years the elk population blew up in this region. That's primarily why these mountains were chosen to bring back wolves. I can't get the ranchers to see how their grazing lands are as threatened by overpopulation of deer and elk as by a small pack of wolves."

"This isn't the only area for such an experiment, right?"

"Our projects are mainly in Arizona and New Mexico. But other wolf programs are in many states. The Mexican gray I'm working with is the rarest of all formerly extinct gray wolf subspecies. They were on the endangered list for forty years."

"Were wolves lost due to expanded ranching?"

"They were hunted out in areas that were taken over by city expansion, recreation and camping, and sport hunters. Ranchers are the loudest objectors to repatriation."

"Interesting. Is that why you decided to become a wildlife biologist?"

"I always had an affinity for wild animals. In college I thought maybe I'd work at some kind of wildlife zoo. Two summers between classes I volunteered at national parks, educating campers on how to keep bears from bothering them. And I helped relocate bears that wandered into campsites."

"Wow, sounds like quite a big job for a college student."

"Yep, but all that experience led to state Game and Fish offering me a job when I graduated. I've always been footloose, so it suited my lifestyle when they sent me to restock lakes with fish, clear trails at wildlife refuges, and I even manned different state park visitors centers off and on."

"Oh, I assumed you'd always worked with wolves."

"No. No matter what you do for Game and Fish, it's rare to stay long in one location."

Tandy drank more coffee. "I had no idea you'd jumped around as much as I did in the military. Is that why you aren't married?"

Wyatt slanted her a wry look. "A nomadic life didn't prevent you from marriage."

"It should have. And yet I wouldn't trade Scotty." She glanced over her shoulder.

"Trade me for what?" asked a muffled voice from the back seat, punctuated by a yawn.

"I wouldn't trade you for anything," Tandy hastened to say. "Did you get any sleep or has our talking kept you awake?"

"I slept. Now I woke up. Mama, will you read me the wolf book?"

"Sure." She set her mug in the console holder and dug the book out of a tote at her feet. "You got through chapter one, right?"

"Yes," Wyatt answered.

She began to read about wolves living in mid- to higher-level forests. The current page listed juniper, pinyon and ponderosa pine. "We're in ponderosa pine right now," she added, pointing out the window.

"Hey! Look over there—is that snow?" Scotty asked, pointing at the trees.

"Yep," Wyatt said with a grin. "And more is beginning to fall from the sky."

Tandy and Scotty both pressed their foreheads to their windows. "Oh, boy, can I touch it?" Scotty flung off his blanket and leaned forward to speak near Wyatt's ear.

"I've a feeling from the way it's coming down it'll stick. Let's drive another twenty or so miles to the top of the pass. Then we can get out and build a snowman if you'd like."

"Goody, goody." Scotty clapped loudly, causing Mr. Bones to wake up and bark.

"Calm down," Tandy ordered. "Scotty has a hood on his jacket. I packed gloves thinking we might need them at the ranch, but what if we all get wet?"

"There's the SUV heater. I figured on stopping for lunch once we're in New Mexico. The restaurant is halfway to Loki's ranch near Silver City. We'll have time to dry off."

"It's been twenty years since I played in snow. It should be fun," she said, warming to the idea. "Until you stop I may as well continue reading."

Scotty agreed, so she opened the book again. "'If fed by humans, like bears, foxes and coyotes, wolves can become a bother to people and pets. Partly they're susceptible to humans because they travel in packs along foot and horse trails.'" Tandy stopped reading and glanced at Wyatt. "Is that why ranchers see them as such a nuisance?"

"Maybe. It's true they're carnivorous. No one has ever said ranchers don't have legitimate gripes. I keep going back to pointing out ecosystem balance. Wolves lived and thrived in the Southwest prior to the introduction of cattle."

"The next page says studies show wolves don't totally eliminate their prey, but continue to move to different locations."

"What does that mean, Mama?"

"Some of this will make better sense when you're older." She went on to read about wolf families setting up dens and having four to seven babies in a litter. She passed the book back for Scotty to see the pictures of baby wolves.

"They're cute," he said. "Are they soft? How many babies do your wolves have, Wyatt?"

"Our team members who flew a helicopter over the area to try and get a count thinks one pair we released had three pups. The second pair we released a few weeks later may only have two. It's hard to get an accurate count from the air. I hope when I catch up to them I can document a true number."

"I wish I could go with you," Scotty said.

"Absolutely not," Tandy told him. "They probably live in mountains like we're driving through now. It'll be hard enough for Wyatt traveling by himself."

Scotty closed the book and dropped it in the seat. "There's a lot more snow outside. When can we stop and build a snowman?"

"Up ahead there's a place to pull off at an overlook. On a good day we could see towns and ranches in New Mexico. But the weather's too foggy today. Only one other traveler has passed us since we left the ranch. I predict we'll have the overlook to ourselves." Shortly after making the statement, he turned off the highway and stopped inside a flat, walled area deep with pristine snow. "This is it. We need to establish some rules. No climbing on the benches. In fact, we should stay far away from the wall as there's a sharp drop-off beyond it. Tandy, do you need both bags for hats and gloves?"

"No, just the camouflage one. The caps and gloves are in the side zip pocket if you just want to grab them. Are you sure this is a good idea?" she asked, peering at the thickly falling snow.

"Up to you. If we don't take this opportunity, how long before you'll have weather to help Scotty build his first snowman?"

"Good point," she said. "Let's get our gear. Scotty, unbuckle, but snap on Mr. Bones's leash and don't let go of him when we get out. I see what looks like a water faucet where we can tie him up for a few minutes. This will be his first experience with snow, too."

"In snow this deep domestic pets need sweaters and booties," Wyatt said. "While you two zip your coats and put on hats and gloves, I'll take him out for a few minutes."

"I should have realized his coat isn't thick enough for such cold. We could still get snow at the ranch. I'll need to order him winter wear."

As it turned out, Mr. Bones didn't like snow at all. Wyatt swept off a spot on the concrete parking area, but the dog shivered, hopped around, whined and barely did his business before trying to climb back into Wyatt's arms. He carried the wiggling animal back to the SUV.

"He was funny," Scotty said, laughing as he rubbed Mr. Bones's ears then wrapped him in the blanket. "I've seen pictures of snowmen. Show me how to start."

"The snow near those trees isn't as dry so it'll roll up better. Tandy, why don't you and Scotty start there and roll it down this incline for the base. I'll make a smaller ball for his middle. Then you two can do his head while I hunt limbs for arms and rocks for eyes and mouth."

They all set about their assigned tasks and soon they were giggling.

"This is funner than building sand castles at the beach," Scotty declared as soon as the snowman really took shape. "When he's done, Mama, will you take a picture of me and him on your phone? I wanna call Mark and send it to him."

Tandy really was enjoying herself more than she'd anticipated. Scotty's request sobered her. She remembered her sister-in-law said the kids shouldn't correspond. *Too bad.* "Sure, I'll take a couple of photos. You can send them to Mark after we head out again."

The snow had slacked off to fine intermittent flakes. The snowman was finished and Scotty declared him "cool," which made them all snicker.

"Okay, Scotty, go stand beside him," Tandy said, digging out her phone.

"Wait." Wyatt held up a hand. "He needs a hat to show he's a cowboy snowman." As he said it, he removed his gray Stetson and set it atop the icy head.

"That's perfect." Tandy snapped a couple of pictures then passed the camera to Scotty. "Go get in the SUV. I'll be right there."

He happily plodded off, but just as Wyatt reached

for his hat she scooped up a snowball and hit him in the back of his neck.

He jumped and tried to dig the wet snow out from inside his collar. "Okay, you're gonna get it now," he called when hearing her chortling.

She backed up fast, but her feet flew out from under her.

Leaving his hat on the snowman, Wyatt made a dive for Tandy. In spite of him reaching her and grabbing hold of her jacket, she fell and so did he. Together they hit the snow and rolled down the incline toward the road.

Both sputtered and teased each other as they sat up and tried brushing off snow clinging to their jackets and jeans.

First to rise, Wyatt extended his hand to help Tandy, who kept slipping as she attempted to stand. He latched on to one of her gloved hands and pulled her upright.

She literally fell into his arms. Instead of releasing her, he tightened his hold, bent his head and kissed her laughing lips.

She struggled for a minute to keep her balance then slid her free arm around his shoulder and kissed him back. Instant heat arced between them, melting the lingering snow from their foreheads, cheeks and chins.

Hearing Scotty holler from the vehicle ended their kiss.

Tandy looked aghast. "Maybe we shouldn't have done that." They were still connected by their fingers.

"But…you looked so kissable." He smiled down at her.

"Hardly," she scoffed. "We both look like abominable snow people." She started up the incline, but her slick-bottomed boots slid and she would have fallen again if Wyatt hadn't thrown his free arm around her waist.

"Let's take this slow and easy," he said, edging up the icy slant. "I'll help you into your seat before I rescue my hat. Don't go getting huffy. Remember who started the snowball fight."

This time her eyes sparkled mischievously as her lips twitched into a smile. "I couldn't resist. What did you think of my aim?"

"Deadeye Dick from my biased aspect," he murmured. He helped her in then dashed back for his hat.

"Mama, did you get hurt?" Scotty had climbed out of his booster and scooted across the back seat. Now he sounded anxious.

"No, honey. I hit Wyatt with a snowball, then in trying to get away from him my feet went out from under me. But I'm fine."

"You hurt your face. I saw him kiss your owie."

"Ah. Uh…" Tandy continued to stammer as Wyatt dropped his hat on the console, settled into his seat and winked.

"I guess you couldn't see from here, sport," he said. "I was checking her over real close to see she hadn't hurt herself. Can you buckle up, or do you need help?"

"I can do it," he said, and did just that. "I can't find Mark's number. And I don't know what to poke to send him a picture. You got great ones of me 'n my snowman."

"I'll set it up, but you can only talk a minute because we're leaving and reception may be bad. Also, if you say we're going to New Mexico, just tell Mark it's to buy a bull. Don't mention we're going with Wyatt."

"Why not?"

Heaving a sigh, she unzipped her jacket and made sure he was secured. She decided not to beat about the bush. "Aunt Lucinda said your father and his new wife are living there now. That makes our contacting them awkward."

"Dad's not nice."

Wyatt's ears perked up. He tried to be discreet, however. He started the engine and backed out of the lookout area so as not to disturb Scotty's snowman.

"I'm sorry. Some day you both may want a better relationship. Do you know what *cordial* is?"

"Nope."

"It means be pleasant. However, what we do now is our business and none of his. Do you understand?"

"Uh-huh. Maybe I won't tell Mark we're going to New Mexico to buy a bull."

"You know what, Scotty? Tell Mark anything you want. Tell him we're going with Wyatt to buy a bull." Tandy completed setting up the call and caught Wyatt's eye when she handed her son the phone.

He smiled and immediately paid attention to driving over the snowy summit.

Tandy had put the phone on speaker and Mark answered on the first ring. "Hi, Scotty. Wow, you got to make a real snowman? I bet playing in snow was fun.

I wish I could visit. Maybe next time you have snow I can. Oh, hey, I can't talk anymore. Mom's yelling at me to come for dinner. Bye, Scotty."

Tandy disconnected the call. "Speaking of eating," Wyatt said, "the place I thought we could stop for lunch is down the hill and around a couple of bends. No more than eight miles."

"I'm hungry. Snowman building is hard. I'm glad we stopped. But I like the heat you turned on. Now I don't gotta take my blanket back from Mr. Bones."

"Don't have to, or don't need to, Scotty," his mother corrected. "You'll be in first grade next year and teachers won't be happy to hear you use bad grammar."

"Will I like school? Wyatt, did you like school?"

"I did."

Tandy shot him a grateful glance.

Taking one hand off the steering wheel, he reached across the console and captured her cold fingers and squeezed. They traded radiant smiles, and he felt his heart quicken when Tandy didn't tug loose. He felt blessed that the road was dry and straight. He didn't need to unclasp from her until he reached the burger place and had to use both of his hands to turn off the highway into the restaurant parking lot.

THEY GOT BACK underway after enjoying hamburgers and the break in a warm place. Wyatt took time to phone Loki and let him know approximately when they'd arrive while Tandy gave Mr. Bones kibble, water and walked him around the restaurant.

"Time to roll," he said once it appeared all were

ready. "My friend and his wife have invited us to join them for supper. I hope we get there in daylight so I can show you around his ranch."

"Will I have time to play with his kids?" Scotty asked.

"Unless for some reason we hit heavier traffic than normal. I always stop at a variety store and pick up a small toy for each of the three kids. You can help me choose this time, and we'll get you something, too," he told Scotty.

"Cool." Scotty bounced in his seat. "I like going places with you, Wyatt. Mama's the only one who ever bought me hamburgers or toys before. But you don't hafta get me anything. You gave me the wolf book and poster."

Tandy spun around. "Didn't Aunt Lucinda or your dad take you for hamburgers or to movies?"

"Nope. Daddy only came if Uncle Dave was there. They went to ball games or did surfing and stuff. Aunt Lucinda only took Mark to school and bought him DVDs."

"What's wrong?" Wyatt noticed Tandy frowning.

"Only that I paid her extra for movies and meals out. I assumed... Obviously I didn't ask enough questions," she added, her frown deepening.

"You're not to blame for what you didn't know, Tandy."

"Thanks. It's a crying shame Dan wasn't more like you."

Wyatt's chest expanded. Not knowing what to say, he reached for her hand again and was rewarded when her frown disappeared.

Chapter Six

They arrived at Loki's ranch midafternoon. Tandy noticed at once an iron arch over metal fencing. The arch had carved words: Pitchfork Ranch. Real pitchforks formed the upright posts holding up the arch. Neat fencing segregated the ranch road from fat cattle grazing on grass wet with dew. The animals were big like her Santa Gertrudis, but buff colored to a darker tan. Her heifers' coats were russet.

"What I wouldn't give to have all this flat land at my ranch," she said, leaning forward to take in more of their surroundings.

"Yeah, this is nice. Loki bought his first two hundred acres with funds earned as a cowhand. Little by little he's expanded to twelve hundred acres. His family helped build his house, barns and the cabin. I took some vacation and swung a hammer, too."

He'd pulled up in front of a log house with a wide porch running the full width. Smoke curled from a stone chimney. They had barely stopped when the front door flew open and two adults, three kids and several dogs piled out. They were hugging all over Wyatt seconds after he exited the SUV. The kids hopped up and down excitedly, calling him Uncle Wyatt.

Despite that Wyatt said she was welcome here, she couldn't help but feel like she and Scotty were intruding on a special reunion. She deliberately held back until Wyatt opened the back door, helped Scotty and Mr. Bones out, and motioned to her.

Wyatt introduced Tandy and Scotty to the Branchwaters. Right off the bat afterward, Loki poked Wyatt in the ribs and said teasingly, "You made it sound as if your landlady was, uh, older." Loki jabbed him again. "But who can blame you for wanting to keep such an attractive woman private?"

"Stop! You're embarrassing me and Tandy. Abby, tell him to mind his manners."

The woman with fine features and long dark hair only rolled her eyes. Hooking an arm through Tandy's she said, "Ignore them. Men are such cretins. Let's go inside out of the chill."

The ranch dogs sniffed Mr. Bones, and the children were already petting him and eyeing Scotty like kids in new situations did.

"Wait." Wyatt held up a hand. "Tandy needs to see the bulls while it's still light. You can tour the house later when Loki and I go trade my SUV," he said.

"Then let's unload our bags now," Tandy said. "Can we set them on the porch?"

"Of course," Abby said.

"And you bought presents," Scotty whispered loudly to Wyatt.

"That I did." He went to the rear of the SUV and set out the duffels, which Tandy picked up. He then handed Scotty a sack with the kids' gifts. "Would you like to give these out? You know who gets what since you helped me choose."

An anxious look crossed the boy's face. "What if they don't like 'em?"

Wyatt dropped to one knee. "Hey, hey. They will. And they'll like you." He brushed his knuckles along Scotty's jaw. "Just be you."

A sunny smile returned. The boy took the bag and hustled around to the front of the vehicles, where the family still huddled. Loki, however, had come to see if he could help unload. Giving Wyatt a hand up, he said in a low voice, "You're an ace faux uncle, but you're a natural-born dad. Past time you get busy on that, bro."

Instead of smacking his best friend, Wyatt surprised himself by saying, "You may be right."

His friend grinned. "About damned time. Come on. Let's take your lady out to the pens to pick a bull. We'll see if she buys Stormtrooper or Darth Vader. In case you're wondering, Parker and Sam named them."

"Tandy, Scotty, I hate to rush you, but Loki's ready to show you his stock and time's ticking past."

It ended up that Abby Branchwater and her brood elected to go along with them to see the bulls. The boys clutched their action figures and Sonia her stuffed wolf exactly like the one Wyatt chose to buy for Scotty even though he insisted he didn't need a gift. It hadn't been hard to see he coveted the toy.

The boys dashed off ahead. Sonia walked more sedately between Abby and Tandy. Wyatt and Loki brought up the rear with Loki pointing out improvements he'd recently made.

"You've been busy," Wyatt said. "I've only been gone a month."

"When is this project winding down? Will you get to stay here awhile next time?"

"I have yet to locate my full wolf pack. Of course," he quickly added, "I haven't been in Arizona the whole month. First I was sent to the Mojave National Preserve in Nevada to test a stream. It was a watering hole for a lot of suddenly dead and dying wild animals."

"Sounds serious. What did you find? Alkali?" Loki asked.

"I never heard. My job was to draw blood from the animals. Others took water samples. Nevada's wildlife department wanted a second opinion."

Loki swept a hand encompassing dry brown fields they were passing. "My biggest worry now isn't feeding my stock, but water. Another year of drought and I'll have to reduce the size of my herd. Or when I ship this batch to market I may invest in returning bison to this area. My cousin Mason's done that with some success in Wyoming. He claims bison are sturdier and forage better in dry climates."

"We saw green grassland driving in." Wyatt's steps slowed.

"The result of intense targeted watering. There's talk of rationing ranchers by fall."

"It snowed when we came over the pass. Maybe you'll get a good runoff."

"I hope so. I see the kids have reached the bull pens. Parker," he yelled. "Are both bulls out?"

"Mama, Mama, come see," Scotty hollered, swinging his free arm in an effort to rush his mother. "They're big. Both look scarier than the bad man's bull."

"Who is the bad man?" Loki asked as the adults caught up to the boys.

"One of Tandy's neighbors. I'll tell you more about him when we go to trade my SUV. The guy's got it in for my wolf project, too."

Tandy turned as Loki and Wyatt walked up. "I like the Charolais. He resembles my cattle, but with lighter coloring. What are you asking for him?"

He named a price that brought a low "oh" from her.

"Too high? I can shave off another fifty bucks," he said, setting his foot on the lowest rung of the fence around the pen.

"No, to the contrary. It's a third less than I would've paid Stewart Darnell, who won't sell to me, period."

Loki's wife, who still stood next to Tandy, bent close and smiled. "Loki decided to give you the family price right after Wyatt phoned. You're his friend and he's like family."

"I want to be fair. You've no idea how much I appreciate the fact you'll sell to me at all. For whatever reason I'm persona non grata throughout my ranch community."

"The bad man scared me at the meeting," Scotty ventured.

"Then it's settled. Stormtrooper is yours for the price I named. We'll load him whenever you decide to leave. We hope you'll stay a few days," Loki said, sliding an arm around his wife's shoulders. "Honey, Wyatt and I are going to run his SUV to his headquarters. I'll call when we know how long we'll be. That'll give you an idea of when to start fixing supper." Stepping away from Abby, he added, "Have the kids put the travel bags in the cabin. Parker can turn on the heat."

"Not my duffel," Wyatt said. "It's the navy blue one. The cabin only has two bedrooms. One for Tandy and one for Scotty. I'll bunk in the small barn hayloft."

"What?" Tandy spun from the bull pen with a shake of her head. "You never told me anything of the sort or I wouldn't have come along."

"I know. But if I'd told you and you stayed home, I didn't want to be responsible for choosing your bull and having you hate him. It's fine. I've slept there plenty of times."

"Not in the winter," Abby tossed out.

Wyatt shrugged.

Loki's oldest son hopped down off the pen enclosure. "Why can't Scotty borrow one of our sleeping bags and stay in my room like our cousins do?"

"That'd be cool. Can I, Mama?" he asked his mother, who continued to shake her head. "Parker's got video games and extra controllers."

"They're kid approved," Abby added.

"I suppose then. If that works for everyone else." Tandy's unsure gaze flitted from Wyatt to Abby to Loki.

Wyatt had a passing thought that such a scheme

would place him alone with Tandy for an entire evening, which set happy anticipation warming him. A second thought had anxiety coursing in its wake. The transient nature of his job had ruined past romantic connections. Lesser ones than what he'd begun to feel for Tandy.

But Loki grinned again in his needling way, so Wyatt decided what the hell. "If it works for everyone else, it's okay by me. Parker, toss my duffel in one of the cabin bedrooms. Tandy can sort out what Scotty needs before you take her bag. Let's go, Loki." He strode off, leaving his good friend to follow.

"You're not pleased with the arrangement?" Loki asked on reaching the vehicle. "I thought I detected sparks."

"Sparks aplenty. Do you remember how bummed I was after I broke up with Kylie for my job? It's the same. Tandy is looking for grounded."

As they climbed into the SUV and drove out, Loki cocked his head. "You and Kylie had conflicting careers where you both could get moved around. Tandy is situated on a ranch. I see how you look at her. I never saw you make cow eyes at Kylie."

"Cow eyes? I do not." Wyatt huffed indignantly.

Loki laughed from his belly. "Oh, buddy, you do. So tell me about the rancher neighbor who has it in for both of you."

Glad for the opportunity to change the subject, Wyatt launched into what he knew about Preston Hicks and even some of the others in the Cattle and Sheep Ranchers Association. "The old cowboy who works for Tandy used to tend her dad's cattle. He says the ringleader at the association wants to buy her ranch."

"By hook or crook?" Loki murmured. "Sounds as if she needs you in her corner, Wyatt."

Feeling pressured, Wyatt launched into what had happened to his SUV.

BACK AT THE HOUSE, Abby told the kids to take the dogs and go play inside. "I'll show Tandy the cabin and get her settled."

Tandy stayed her son. "Scotty, wait. I should've packed you a separate bag. Here, take your pj's, toothbrush and clean clothes for tomorrow." Unzipping her duffel, she lifted out his things, which he snatched, then he ran off with the others.

"He and Mr. Bones are in hog heaven having your kids and pets to play with," Tandy murmured, hefting her bag after noting Abby held Wyatt's. "Our ranch is so remote." She explained how she'd inherited Spiritridge.

"I hate to ask, but did you lose your husband in the war? Wyatt said you'd both served in the army."

"I'm divorced. Dual deployment puts a strain on relationships, and I'm only finding out it took a toll on Scotty, too. He stayed with my sister-in-law in Honolulu. I thought it was ideal. Her husband was in the navy and away a lot. I expected Scotty's father to co-parent, but he didn't."

"That's awful," Abby exclaimed as she unlocked the cabin. "Wyatt will be good for him. He's wonderful with our kids."

"He's been exceedingly nice to Scotty. Wow, this

cabin is way nicer than my casitas. It's a wonder Wyatt elected to come back and rent from me. As you probably know, he'd rented from my dad when he first set up the wolf project."

"Yes. He really liked your father and felt so bad when he passed away." Abby led the way to bedrooms separated by a Jack and Jill bathroom. She dropped Wyatt's duffel in a room with masculine decor. The second bedroom where Tandy left her bag was still rustic but done in more neutral shades.

"I'll serve breakfast at our house. You and Wyatt will probably want coffee first thing. He knows where the cabin coffee maker's stored." Abby crossed the compact living room and turned up the thermostat. Her cell phone buzzed. "It's Loki," she said, tapping to answer. "Hi, babe. Did you get to town in time to exchange Wyatt's SUV?"

"Yep." Loki's voice boomed into the room. "They gave him a king cab pickup. It has a trailer hitch, so he didn't need to buy one. He suggested we stop at Andy's for fried chicken and all the fixin's so we don't have to cook tonight."

Abby quirked a brow at Tandy, who rotated a shoulder, but then gave a thumbs-up.

"Bless Wyatt. That sounds good. We have soda for the kids, beer for you guys, and wine for Tandy and me, unless she prefers the other." She ended the call, blowing kisses into the phone.

Her easy, loving relationship with her husband stabbed painful regret through Tandy. On returning to the main house she watched all the kids, including Scotty, shout with glee. That was the moment she realized she was open to another relationship. Her bad experience with Dan hadn't totally killed her desire to share her life and Scotty's with a man capable of being a partner and a dad. But it was wrong to picture Wyatt in that role given he was so footloose.

Tandy, who'd had few women pals, found Abby easy to be around. She fed all the dogs, turned on country music, and the women jabbered and laughed like old friends while setting the big dining table.

She was warmed by the camaraderie swirling in this home. The contrast with Lucinda's place in Hawaii was stark. At once she determined with clarity that this was the model she'd emulate. *Someday.*

Ten minutes later the men blew into the house enveloped in yummy odors of fast food so potent it brought the kids pouring out of Parker's bedroom. The sheer joy made Tandy acutely aware of all that had been missing in her marriage.

As everyone crowded around the trestle table, Abby gave Tandy condiments and paper towels to hand out. That made her chuckle and feel even more at home.

The kids yammered and chowed down. Tandy noticed Scotty fit in and didn't hold back. It warmed her heart.

The adults discussed ranching, wild animals and even exchanged recipes. Once the food had been consumed, the kids disappeared to play. The guys escaped to the barn to look at farm implements. Left to clear the table, the women glanced at each other and laughed. "I guess this is typical," Tandy said, tossing the paper plates in the trash. She shared her experience with big meals in the military. "Any time we ate at base camp it was bedlam."

"You're amazing," Abby said. "I can't imagine fighting a war or running a cattle ranch on my own. If anything ever happened to Loki, I'd sell the ranch and move in with family, I guess."

"I got out of the army to make a home for Scotty. I was an only child as were my folks. I'm disheartened that neighbors kept me from purchasing a bull and from hiring an able-bodied helper." Tandy relayed her fears about Manny's health and how he'd come out of retirement for her.

Tandy's cell phone rang just as the men stomped back into the house. She peered at the readout, gasped and said to Wyatt, "It's Manny." Rushing to a quiet alcove, she answered.

"Tandy, I hate like the devil to bother you, but the south fence has two sections down. Preston's heifers have swarmed into your pasture. His cows are lined up for a quarter mile drinking from your stream. It's like they're starved for water."

"So he cut our wire again?"

"That's the heck of it. Those sections were knocked down from the inside. Hicks pointed that out when I called him to complain. After he learned you were away, he ignored me. He's not driving his cows home. What should I do?"

"What can you do but keep watch? I've bought a bull. Wyatt's swapped his vehicle. We'll head home at first light." She cast a worried glance at him for confirmation.

He bobbed his head and Tandy signed off with

Manny. "I'm so sorry," she said to the others. "We'd all love to stay longer, but I have fence down and the neighbor isn't cooperating with removing his cattle."

Abby rounded the table. "If you need to leave early, we'd better get the kids to bed."

"Please don't disrupt their schedule on my account. Scotty can sleep on the drive home. I'll go to the cabin and grab some shut-eye so I can drive the first leg. Wyatt, you stay and catch up with your friends. I'm so sorry." Tandy collected her jacket and went to advise Scotty.

"I'll turn in, too. I can't let anyone else drive a government vehicle." Wyatt hugged Abby and lightly punched Loki's shoulder. Shrugging into his jacket, he waited for Tandy by the door.

"Breakfast at five a.m," Abby announced.

Exiting Parker's bedroom, Tandy exclaimed, "We can't put you out like that."

"It won't be the first breakfast I've cooked at dawn. It's daily at roundup."

Loki trailed them onto the porch. "We'll eat then load the bull. And let me know what happens with the neighbor. He sounds like a real SOB."

Agreeing, Wyatt followed Tandy to the steps and helped her with her jacket. Their path went dark when Loki shut the door, so Wyatt kept his arm around Tandy until they reached the cabin.

"It's cold in here," he noted. "There's a gas fire-place. I'll turn it on for a while."

"Abby turned on the heat. But, you're right. Maybe I'll sit in front of it a few minutes to warm up. I feel horrid for cutting our trip short. Your friends are so nice."

Once he got the blaze going, Wyatt sat on the couch and patted the cushion beside him. "I wish your spring pasture didn't border Hicks's land. His behavior concerns me."

"Me, too. Thanks to Dad, though, the lease is paid up and I have ten years left on it." Tandy sat, kicked off her boots and curled her feet under her.

Deftly sliding closer, Wyatt cuddled her into the crook of his arm and rested his chin on top of her hair. "You could talk to Loki and ask if one of his many cousins might work for you when my project ends. They've all grown up wrangling cattle."

"It's a thought. I wish I knew why I'm such a pariah." She raised her head to look at Wyatt and he bent swiftly and kissed her.

She pressed against him, returning his kiss and, after a moment, touched his cheek.

When neither one could breathe, he broke their lip-lock. But his heated gaze never veered from her slumberous eyes.

"This isn't smart," she murmured.

"I like kissing you. Are you upset?"

"No." She gave a small shake of her head. "Everyone wants to be kissed."

He smiled softly and pulled her onto his lap, where he kissed her again. A kiss that went deeper and lasted longer.

It lasted so long her fingers curled into the fabric of his shirt. Once the kiss mutually ended, Tandy loosened a hand and ran a tentative finger over his lips. "This could easily lead to more. But, we have to be realistic."

"How so?"

"I have big obligations. Namely a son and a ranch."

"Neither of which I'd do anything to hurt."

She sighed. "You're a good man. I know you'd never mean to hurt me or Scotty. But we both know your job is going to take you away. I can't do a one-night stand. Or even one week or one month."

Closing his eyes, Wyatt set his forehead against hers. "Didn't some wise person say where there's a will there's a way? I can promise you tonight."

"And it's so tempting." Tandy flattened a hand against his chest where she could feel his racing heart matched the tempo of her own. "You're such a wonderful man, I could probably guilt you into promising you'd stay. I can't do that." A trail of tears leaked from her eyes and he kissed them away.

"I'm warm. You're warmer. And this is cozy," she said, pulling back. "Dawn comes early. We both need sleep." Climbing off his lap, she opened her mouth to say more, but couldn't find the words. Instead she ran into her room and firmly shut the door.

"I shouldn't be objecting," Wyatt murmured to her closed door.

IN THE MORNING they had a lot to do in a short amount of time. Avoiding Wyatt, Tandy helped clean up after breakfast while the men went out to load Storm-trooper.

"I wish we didn't hafta leave," Scotty lamented. "Mama, put Parker's number in your phone."

Tandy set up the contact as Wyatt installed Scotty's booster seat in his pickup. "I wish we had more time, too." And that was true. But she and Scotty said their goodbyes and went out just as the men closed up the trailer's tailgate.

Loki said, "If I decide to raise bison, come back and see if you think they'd do better on your ranch, Tandy."

She nodded, thinking the likelihood of that happening was slim to none once Wyatt finished with his wolves and left Spiritridge. She lifted her sleepy son and Mr. Bones into their seats.

Loki and Wyatt shook hands, slapped shoulders, then Loki joined his family on the porch.

Everyone waved heartily. And Wyatt drove out as salmon streaks bathed the home and family they'd left behind in warm pink light.

Tandy turned on the radio. It wasn't long before Mr. Bones and Scotty fell asleep. She expected Wyatt to mention last night's interlude, but he said nothing. She'd been prepared to voice some possibilities for advancing their relationship. His silence on the subject left her unsure of herself. She couldn't tell where he stood—maybe he'd thought it over and concluded that it wouldn't work.

On reaching the top of the pass Wyatt drove into a snowstorm the likes of which Tandy had never experienced. Worried about a restless, bawling bull threatening to kick the sides out of their trailer killed any thought of romance.

It began to thunder. Lightning forked through falling snow. Tandy gripped Wyatt's arm. "What's happening? Shouldn't we pull off under the trees and wait this out?"

"It's thundersnow," he returned through gritted teeth. "See the hail mixed with the snow that's beginning to freeze on the windshield? We need to drive on before the road gets too slick to travel."

"I've never heard of thundersnow."

Scotty woke up when Mr. Bones howled as only a hound could do. "What's hitting my window?" He jerked forward. "When we made the snowman, the snow was soft."

"It's called hail," Tandy said. "Growing up in Hawaii, you've never seen hail."

"Thundersnow is a rare occurrence." Wyatt adjusted the defroster. "The department covered it in a training class. It takes elevated instability and strong dynamic lift in the atmosphere along with colder troposphere. Below freezing."

"Okay. Sorry I asked." Tandy handed Scotty his stuffed wolf.

"Where's my snowman?" The boy pressed his nose to the side window. "I want to stop and make another one."

A bolt of lightning hit to the right of the front fender. Everyone jumped at the sight.

"Scotty, we've passed the overlook where we built your snowman. Even if we hadn't, the weather's too dangerous. Can you pet Mr. Bones to keep him calm?"

"I will, Mama. But don't be scared. Wyatt's gonna keep us safe."

"I'm scared the bull will break a leg."

"Hang tough for fifteen minutes. We'll be off the

mountain and into the valley, where the hail and snow will hopefully turn to rain," Wyatt said.

He was correct. Ten minutes later the pinging on the cab roof stopped as did Stormtrooper's banging around. But rain continued to beat down.

Tandy unclenched her hands to pour Wyatt and herself coffee Abby had provided. She filled a travel mug with hot chocolate for Scotty.

Once his cup was dry, Wyatt glanced at Tandy. "How close can I drive to the pasture where you want to offload the bull? The rain slacked so we should do it as soon as we get to the ranch."

"I'd hoped to turn him in with my heifers straight-away. There's a fire road that ends ten yards from my back gate." She sawed her lip between her teeth. "Wait, is that a dumb idea if two sections of my fence are down and Preston's cows are overrunning my lease?"

"Call Manny. Ask if we should put him in the corral behind the barn. Sometimes he lets the horses run there. If they're loose we need a plan B."

She took out her phone. "Are we an hour out from the ranch?"

"Barring this rain worsening, maybe an hour and a half."

Tandy tapped her cell. When Manny answered, she laid out their situation and ETA.

"Tandy, I tried to call you earlier. I got nothing so figured you were out of cell range. You won't believe what I found at the lease this morning. Hicks's cows were all gone. I swear even their hoofprints. The fence sections are in place. It's as if I dreamed the whole thing. 'Cept I know I didn't."

"That's totally weird. If all is back to normal, we'll drive to the south gate on the fire road and offload the bull. If you, Wyatt and I form a triangle around him, I think we can drive him from the road to pasture with no problem. Where are you?"

"I just picked up a prescription in town. I'll go to the ranch, saddle a horse and meet you there. Give me an hour."

"Wyatt says we're an hour and a half out. Is it raining at the ranch?"

"Has been. The storm's blown by, but the fire road will be muddy. Don't get stuck. See ya, kid."

"You heard?" she said to Wyatt.

"I agree it's weird. What it tells me is that Preston Hicks is up to something. I wish we knew what."

"No good where I'm concerned. Maybe he's messing with our minds."

"I don't like him, Mama," Scotty said from the back seat.

"I know, honey. I'm not overly fond of him myself. Thinking back to when I was a kid, he and Dad often lent each other a hand. And his wife did a lot when my mom was sick and then died. He's changed."

"I'm hungry," Scotty whined. "Can we get pizza for lunch?"

"We don't want to drive into town pulling Stormtrooper in the trailer. Can you wait until we get him settled?" Tandy asked. "Then we'll go home and I'll fix us all tomato soup and grilled cheese sandwiches."

"I s'ose."

"Thanks, buddy." Wyatt glanced at the boy through the rearview mirror. "The rain has tapered off. The ground by the corral will be perfect to spot tracks. I'll take you out after lunch and you can show me what you find."

"Goody, goody! Did you know Parker can track? He and his dad followed coyotes that were killing their chickens. They caught 'em and called your office, Wyatt. Guys came and took the coyotes somewhere far away."

"That's a major job of Game and Fish. Help coexistence between ranchers, farmers and wild animals."

"Is that what you're gonna do with the wolves and those guys who were mean to Mama?"

"Lord willing," he said around a hefty expelled breath.

With the fire road muddier than expected, Wyatt had to slow down. They bounced over deep ruts.

Manny awaited them on horseback at the end of the road.

"Scotty, I want you and Mr. Bones to stay in the pickup while we move Stormtrooper."

"Aww, why can't I help?"

"It's really important that you keep Mr. Bones from barking and scaring the bull," Wyatt told the boy.

"Okay."

Tandy climbed out. "Manny, did you open the gate?"

"Not yet. Didn't want the heifers running out. I'll do it now." He rode off.

Wyatt joined Tandy at the back of the trailer.

"You always seem to say the right thing to Scotty. He was building up to pitch a fit over my telling him to stay in the cab."

"I don't mean to step on your toes. He's eager to help so I suggested a job."

"I admire your quick thinking," she said as she unlocked the trailer.

Talk stopped when Manny returned on foot. "I tied my horse to a tree. Let's get this bad boy on his way. He's a beauty," the old cowboy said, stepping aside as Wyatt backed the big animal down the ramp. "See his nostrils flare? He smells the heifers, some of whom are in heat. Driving him into the pen's gonna be a snap."

And he was right. The three formed their triangle, but the bull beelined through the open gate. Manny started to swing it shut.

Wyatt stayed him. "Wait a sec. I want to see where you say the fence was down. Tandy, close the gate behind me. I'll climb over when I come back. I'm interested to see why there are no tracks."

"Can Scotty go, too?" Tandy posed the question to Wyatt.

"Sure. You keep the dog leashed. This won't take long. I know everyone's hungry."

Tandy motioned to her son, who eagerly joined them. She took Mr. Bones's leash.

Scotty happily smiled at his mom and casually slipped his hand in Wyatt's. The pair followed Manny over a footbridge and he pointed out the two sections.

Wyatt bent to inspect them. "If you hadn't told me these were down yesterday, I'd have missed seeing these wood chips around the post bases. Someone recently worked on this fence."

"I counted at least eighty head of Hicks's cows along the stream on Tandy's lease. Do you see hoof-prints anywhere along the muddy bank?"

"I don't," Scotty said.

The boy scrambled alongside Wyatt as he walked a short distance then returned to say, "I believe some-one dragged burlap over the ground before it rained." Going to the fence, Wyatt vaulted across. "Come see this." He hoisted Scotty over and let Manny traverse on his own.

"What are we looking at?" the old man asked, puffing as he glanced around.

Taking out his cell phone, Wyatt shot photos of the ground. "No tracks on Tandy's lease, but plenty here. All run the width of the double fence section." He straightened. "Look closely. All tracks lead away from the stream, uphill to Hicks's ranch. And here, three sets of boots. So three people were involved. Question is, why?"

Manny shook his head.

Scotty said, "Gosh, Wyatt, now I see, too. Was one the bad man?"

"I don't know." They walked back and he boosted Scotty back over the fence, then he assisted Manny before climbing back himself. They recrossed the footbridge. "Tandy said maybe Preston is trying to mess with your minds. Tomorrow I've got to trail my wolves. It'll be up to you three to watch for anything else out of the ordinary."

Hearing Wyatt's last edict, Tandy hugged him and

Manny. "I'm lucky you two have my back. The most I can offer by way of thanks is lunch." To her surprise, Manny also accepted.

Chapter Seven

Wyatt loaded his backpack with equipment and left the next morning moments before light illuminated the peaks. He drove to a spot where the road ended at a campground. In full but cloudy daylight, he set out on foot to find his wolf pack.

His mind was only partly on his mission because his thoughts kept drifting to yesterday at Tandy's. A simple meal of soup and sandwiches shouldn't have felt special, but it had. Perhaps it was the family atmosphere. They'd all talked and joked while eating. Scotty filled Manny in on the trip.

After supper Wyatt had helped Tandy clear the table and load the dishwasher while Manny, like a grandfather, retired to the living room and taught Scotty to play checkers. Looking back, it was as if Tandy and he could've been married. In fact, he'd stolen a kiss and she hadn't pushed him away.

His own family had been so fractured. His grandmother had provided a roof over his head and food in his belly, but she'd never welcomed his friends. So it'd be a stretch to call her old house home. He wanted more when he settled down.

As he wove through underbrush looking for wolf tracks, it struck him that he'd always wanted more.

What if that more was Tandy and Scotty and he left it all behind for his job? If he tossed in Manny as a grandpa, the scale tilted ever more one-sided.

On the other side of the scale were wolf projects in numerous states. The fact Scotty begged to go with him in search of the pack seemed to him what most boys would do. It's what he did as a boy. But he could tell Scotty's insistence frightened Tandy. Maybe he needed to taper off their tracking practices.

He ran across the first wolf signs and stuffed all prior thoughts into a corner. The pack had moved lower than was safe for them or for ranchers' cattle. Quite likely the late snowfall, especially with thunder and lightning, had driven one or both families down the mountain in search of food and shelter.

He came to a clearing where wolves had fed on an elderly elk. Softening his steps, he readied his dart gun seconds before his homing device went crazy. Noting tracks curving around a boulder, he followed them and sighted a collared male, a female and three pups. He tranquilized the adults, but took care to remain vigilant for the second pair. He thought four adults had fed at the downed elk.

The pups were too cute. All appeared healthy. He took photos, replaced radio telemetry collars on the adults and installed them on the youngsters after vaccinations. Retreating deeper into the woods, he climbed a tree to wait. From this perch he could be sure the tranquilized animals woke up.

All at once his phone rang. The tune blared loudly

in the silent forest and scared a couple of woodpeckers from an adjacent tree. It wasn't easy finding the phone in his pack while perched in a tree fork.

Seeing Tandy's number in the readout, his stomach balled. He imagined she'd only disturb him at his work if something bad had happened. "Tandy, what's wrong?" he demanded, trying to watch the wolves while curbing his panic.

"Where are you?" She was plainly trying to whisper.

"A mile and a half off the hiking trail above Eagle Creek. Why?"

"Preston Hicks and two men are at my lease looking for you. They claim a wolf killed one of Rollie Jefferies's heifers this morning. Scotty's beside himself over them ranting that you have to leave and they're going to rid the area of the wolves."

"Where is the Jefferies ranch?" Wyatt's stomach bottomed out, not in fear for himself, but his second wolf family.

"A good twenty miles south of Spiritridge." She gave him directions.

"Okay. I'll go see what's up. Tell Scotty the wolves in my program are protected by law." He didn't add, unless the wolf was caught eating a domestic animal. He knew the threat of fines or even jail time wasn't guaranteed to save wolves from irate ranchers, but it should calm Scotty. "Can you ask those guys to contact Jefferies? I don't want him disturbing the cow or anything around it until I examine the site. If he's right, I have a form he needs to fill out for a government subsidy."

"How long will you be? I'll meet you there."

"No, Tandy. We don't want Scotty viewing a mangled heifer. And you should act like I'm only your renter."

"But…you're more, Wyatt. Really, I thought you knew."

"Ah… I'm glad. But I've seen ranchers with bloodlust against our wildlife programs before. I want you to stay safe."

"I'm not a helpless female in need of protection. I earned a sharpshooter badge every year I was in the army, so they don't scare me."

"Except Hicks isn't rational. Don't tell them, but I'm waiting for adult wolves to wake up. I had to tranquilize them to vaccinate some pups. I can probably get to the Jefferies ranch by noon."

"Okay, but will you be in danger? Should I notify Sheriff Anderson?"

"Don't worry. They talk big, but they all know I represent a government agency with power to jail them. I'll call you when I arrive and when I leave the Jefferies ranch, okay?"

"That will have to do, but it doesn't mean I won't worry."

"I like that," he said, lowering his voice and hopefully injecting deep appreciation in his response. "It's been a long time since anyone worried about me."

"Bye for now, and please take care."

"I will." Wyatt slid his phone back into the pack, happy to see his two wolves were up and walking. Quick to shake off the effects, it was obvious they picked up his human scent. Herding the pups, they raced away.

He watched them flee to higher ground before he climbed from the tree and hiked to where he'd parked. With Tandy's directions he was sure he could drive straight to the Jefferies ranch. Experiencing a renewed warmth, he smiled to himself, backed around and bounced onto the main highway.

Wyatt expected to be met by a committee of disgruntled men from the Cattle and Sheep Ranchers Association. But Rollie paced alone in front of his home.

Before exiting his pickup, Wyatt phoned Tandy to say he'd arrived. Then he grabbed a clipboard, his camera and prepared to speak to an unhappy rancher.

"Ms. Graham told Pres you wanted to see the wolf kill. I don't know why. It's plain to me it wasn't a mountain lion. They break a heifer's neck. This poor cow had her throat ripped out. I want to cut it up and save the meat. Good you came when you did or I'd have had it butchered."

"I brought a form for restitution. It requires attached photos, which is why I'm here."

"Then follow me."

They crossed rolling knolls of grass all awash in grazing cattle. No sign of snow this far down the mountain. "Nice ranch," Wyatt commented.

"I think so. I need every cow and calf to live so I can pay my property taxes," Jefferies said, his tone surly.

"I understand. The government pays twice market value."

"So I heard." The man Wyatt followed stopped by

a dead, partially butchered heifer. Wyatt took note of the hindquarters in a farm wagon. The carcass lay between a small stream and a line of cottonwoods. Wyatt uncapped his camera and began shooting. He took close-ups of tracks pressed into damp earth. There were some not occluded by Rollie's boots.

"Terrible carnage," the owner said.

"Did you show up and scare off the intruder?"

"Nope. I came out at six a.m. and spotted a downed cow, so I rode over."

"This kill happened earlier. Blood's coagulated. It's odd the wolf or wolves didn't feed."

Rollie shrugged. "I wouldn't know anything about that. Let me fill out the form to be paid for my loss."

Wyatt handed him the clipboard, but he remained bothered by paw prints half the size of his fist. Squatting by a set of clear tracks, he casually asked, "Have you seen or heard of any hybrid wolf dogs in the county?"

The man stopped writing. "Are you trying to screw me out of payment or is this about getting your killer wolves off the hook?"

Rising, Wyatt shook his head. "I just turn in the report. Someone in the department decides on payment."

The rancher glared but completed the form without another word. He shoved the board back at Wyatt.

"I'll go send this to my office." Wyatt tipped his hat and started back the way they'd come all the while judging how far this was from his two wolf packs.

Jefferies caught up. "The association board met last night. We voted to ban Ms. Graham from market. No feedlot will accommodate her as long as she rents to you."

Wyatt tried not to break stride when his spine stiffened. He'd like to punch the jerk, but that wouldn't help Tandy's cause. "I rented from her dad. No one stopped Manny Vasquez and me from selling his cattle at market."

"The sergeant's different. Preston would've paid top dollar to buy Curt's ranch. She didn't have the sense to take the deal. Plus, she was warned to not rent to you but ignored us. That makes her enemy number two. You being number one."

"She's no longer a sergeant. She's a fellow rancher. I should think you'd all respect her service to the country."

Jefferies lip curled and he veered off, leaving Wyatt alone to fume.

Driving back to Spiritridge, he knew in his bones Jefferies's heifer hadn't been killed by a wolf. One pair may not have been at Eagle Crest today, but there were no pup tracks around that heifer. Only hungry wolves killed. There was no sign of feeding.

TANDY RAN OUT of the house to meet Wyatt moments after he pulled in. "I've been worried sick," she called, rushing up as he climbed from the cab. "You phoned to say you were at Rollie's, but you promised to call when you left, too."

"Sorry, I forgot." Lacing a hand around her neck, he drew her in for a kiss. Loosening his hold, he nibbled his way to her ear, nipped it lightly then returned to her mouth to kiss her again.

She blinked when he finally released her. "Wow! What was that for?"

"Part apology for not calling. I told you I'm not used to anyone caring about my whereabouts. To be honest, I suppose it's a bit of frustration, too, for a situation beyond my control."

"So I take it one of your wolves killed a cow."

"Rollie thinks so. My packs are miles from his ranch. His heifer had the earmarks of a wolf kill. But tracks around the animal are larger than any of mine. We weigh, measure and document size before release. I think there are hybrids in the area. Could be part wolf and German shepherd or husky. Manny said he hasn't seen any ranch dogs matching that description. Have you?"

She shook her head. "Most ranchers own herd dogs. I'm probably the only one with a pet. Oh, here comes Scotty. I'd rather not discuss this in front of him."

"I agree. I need to go send in Rollie's claim and my photos."

Scotty flung himself at Wyatt. "I thought those mean men did something awful to you."

"As you see, I'm fine. I only met with the ranch owner. No one else came around." He set the boy down. "I told your mom I have work to do at the cabin."

"But Mama baked chicken and 'vited Manny to supper. You'll come, too, won't you? Yesterday was the funnest ever." The boy clung to his arm.

Wyatt was pretty sure he should refuse based on Rollie's send-off message and that kiss he probably had no business delivering. He could've bitten his tongue when he agreed to join them.

"I had no idea when you'd get home. The chicken will be done at six. Will that give you enough time?" Tandy asked.

"If I get at it. I have photos to take off my camera. And a report to write on the pups I vaccinated today." With that, he went off to his casita to get to work.

Work took Wyatt right up to supper time. He'd used a few minutes to make extra copies of photos of the wolf pups. Those were fine to give Scotty. He ran off a set of the tracks circling the heifer to show Manny. Given how long the old man had been working cattle, maybe he'd seen tracks with the sharp toenail imprint of a wolf. A non-tracker might not think them significant.

On entering Tandy's house, Wyatt again experienced a sense of coming home. His casita was a place to bunk, as was the cabin at Loki's. Here, a crackling fire, comfy furniture, a chattering boy and his yappy dog, combined with Tandy's radiant smile, served as a balm to his lonely heart. An extra heavy one tonight, because it was wrong for him to stay knowing he was why other ranchers had walled her off. She deserved to be accepted as part of the greater ranching community, and her chances of that were better if he didn't stick around. Rollie had made that clear.

Manny came in right behind him, saying, "Tandy, you're spoiling me. Until your dad got sick I never took meals in the main house. Wasn't seemly. Now the smell of your fine cooking reaches across the yard and calls to me."

"What does Mama's cooking say?" Scotty asked, making everyone laugh.

Wyatt set a hand on the lively boy's head. "I bet it says eating family style is way better than sitting alone in front of a TV with something zapped in the microwave."

"And we like company, don't we, Scotty?" Tandy gazed indulgently at her son.

"I wish Wyatt was my daddy and Manny my grandpa like Mark has."

His bold statement caused his mother to blush and had the two men scrabbling for some type of response.

Manny saved them both by hooking a hand over the boy's shoulder as he said earnestly, "Your grandfather was one of the finest men I ever met. A fellow like him is darned near impossible to replace. I'll do my best to honor him by being a family friend."

Scotty looped both arms around the old cowboy, but his gaze cut to Wyatt, more or less waiting for his reply. He was saved from doing so by the sound of the oven buzzer and Tandy announcing, "Supper's done. Take your seats. There's coffee ready. Let me set out the food then I'll pour your milk, Scotty."

Placing sizzling chicken, baked potatoes and cooked carrots in the center of the kitchen table, she said, "Tomorrow night I plan to make chicken chimichangas. I found my mom's recipe. I recall Wyatt mentioning at his friends' home that he liked Abby's chimis. Manny, did you ever eat the ones Mom fixed?"

"I'll say. After I told Mrs. Marsh hers were better than my mother's, she gave me some every time she made them."

"Can I have a chicken leg?" Scotty asked, holding up his plate. "Then can Wyatt tell us about the dead cow?"

"That's not exactly table talk," he said. "I almost forgot. I brought you photographs I took of the wolf pups." He removed the prints from his shirt pocket and set them by Scotty. "I think I've found all the pups, but I'm not totally sure."

"Cool beans." The boy grabbed the pictures. "Parker says that," he added. "What's the other picture you put back in your pocket?"

"Uh, tracks I'll show Manny later." Wyatt held his plate out for Tandy to fill.

"Can I see the tracks?" Scotty talked between bites, insisting he wanted to help Wyatt track any missing pups.

Both his mom and Wyatt said "no" forcefully.

Diverted for a moment, the boy fed Mr. Bones under the table and begged Manny for a game of Go Fish after supper.

"One game," Tandy said. "If Manny can stay. It's later tonight than we usually eat. It's already past your bedtime. Remember, tomorrow we're going to check on our new bull to see how he's getting along with the herd."

Manny pushed back his empty plate. "I have a dental appointment tomorrow morning. But I'm not so sleepy I can't play one game."

Falling into the pattern they'd established the previous evening, Manny and Scotty went in by the fireplace. Tandy and Wyatt cleared the table and rinsed dishes.

It wasn't long, however, before Manny called goodbye and Scotty headed off to bed with his dog.

Wyatt realized he'd missed showing Manny the photo of tracks by the dead heifer.

"What are your plans for tomorrow?" Tandy asked Wyatt, who plucked up his jacket and cowboy hat he'd left by the door.

He thought about saying he needed to see if the motel in town had a room. Instead he said, "I need to double down and locate any remaining pups. Actually, I have to pull up the winter photos our team took from the air to see if I've tagged them all. My pictures will prove our wolf families are nowhere near Jefferies's ranch. Why?"

"No special reason. The coffee's still hot. How about I pour us each another mug? If we wear jackets we can sit on the porch swing and watch the moon rise. It's slated to be full. No rain or snow predicted tonight."

"Okay. I'll pour while you tuck Scotty in and get your coat." Wyatt figured this would give him an opportunity to speak to her about moving to a motel, although the thought ripped pain through his chest.

The size of the porch swing required them to sit close together. Tandy sort of shivered, so Wyatt wrapped an arm around her, molding her against his side. "Are you sure it's warm enough for this?" he asked, leaning down to kiss her nose.

"You didn't seem yourself tonight. I couldn't help

but notice you looked particularly uncomfortable when Scotty said he wished you were his dad. Is that an unsavory notion to you?"

"What? Unsavory?" Rearing back, he gaped at her. "Nothing could be further from the truth." Despite knowing he ought to explain his need to leave, he couldn't let her think that might be a reason. Clearly he'd have to postpone his decision.

"Good." She snuggled closer. "Hypothetically speaking, if you had a stepson Scotty's age, would you want more children?"

"Tandy...wasn't that evident when we were at Loki and Abby's?"

"Loving someone else's children isn't necessarily an indication you'd want a houseful of your own. I thought Dan loved his sister's kids, and too late I realized that didn't mean he wanted his own. I'd never subject Scotty to such humiliation again."

Rubbing his day-old beard over her hair, Wyatt injected a teasing quality to his next question. "Are you by chance proposing to me?"

"Of course not," she said. "I won't lie. Shockingly the possibility has popped into my head. I feel I should confess, rushing into marriage with Dan left me hesitant to trust my feelings again. I do sometimes picture you and me together, but it's fleeting. I doubt that's love. What do you think?"

"You're asking someone who's unsure how to measure love. I know I'd do whatever's necessary to protect you and Scotty."

"That sounds a lot like parenting. I don't need a father, Wyatt. I think I have what it takes to protect myself and Scotty. I hesitate because I know how dedicated you are to your job. Just…forget I said anything."

He settled back and spoke huskily near her ear. "If anyone could tempt me to rethink sticking with Fish and Game, it'd be you and Scotty. The truth is, I love what I do and it's important work." He squeezed her arm gently. "But it does take me all over the place, sometimes without much notice. If we became serious, it'd be too hard to go away all the time. And I'd hate to start a relationship with someone who'd eventually resent me for doing what I love…"

"It's okay, Wyatt. I get it. And, honestly, after Dan, I think Scotty deserves someone who will be around to watch him grow up. I think I deserve that, too." She glanced down briefly before offering him a small smile. "What do you say we let that be enough for now?" She sipped her coffee then rested her temple against his chest.

"Suits me." He took a swig from his mug. "Oh, look, that is a full moon coming up."

They sat entranced by the rise of the icy orb and scattered stars popping out over the casitas to bathe the area in pale light.

Tandy was first to say, "I can tell neither of us wants to move, but we both have busy mornings." She stood and took his empty mug. Even though she had her hands full, after he got to his feet she rose on tiptoes and kissed him. And she stretched up for a second kiss after he opened the screen door to let her go in.

Then pressing her lips against his heart, she murmured, "Good night."

Wyatt wandered slowly back to his rental. What if he didn't move somewhere else? Possibly the ranchers association members were bluffing. But what if they weren't?

Low dark clouds hung over the valley the next morning, totally blocking the mountains. Practically tasting rain, Wyatt tossed his pack in his pickup and wondered if he'd dreamed the full moon and sparkling stars from the night before. If so, he would've invented holding Tandy close, too.

Mr. Bones appeared out of nowhere, darting around his feet. Wyatt swiveled but didn't see anyone at the barn. Then he remembered Manny had a morning appointment in town and Tandy probably wouldn't ride out so early to check the cattle.

He scooped up the wriggling hound, who tried to lick his face, and crossed to the house. He had one foot on the steps leading to the porch when the house door flew open and Scotty emerged calling for his dog.

"I've got him, Scotty. He tried to climb in my pickup. You need to take him into the house because I'm off to hunt my wolves."

The barefoot boy came out in pajamas to claim his pet. "Mama heard the weatherman on TV say it's gonna rain real hard soon. We're not going to the pasture until Manny comes back from his 'pointment. Maybe you shouldn't go up the mountain."

"It's not raining yet. I've seen storm clouds like

this blow over. Remember, I said it's easier to follow tracks when the ground is wet. I'll be fine. You scoot on inside with Mr. Bones." Turning, Wyatt jogged back to his vehicle.

As he headed out he saw Tandy at her door. She smiled and waved to him even as she ushered Scotty and his dog into the house.

Her smile did more in the way of a warm send-off than Wyatt's first swallow of hot coffee from his travel mug. Again he toyed with the idea of lingering on at the ranch. At least until Tandy hired a more able-bodied cowboy to replace Manny. Man, was that a lame excuse. Hiring a new cowhand could take months. Still, what was his big rush to leave? He could stay and interface between his wolves and the ranchers.

Having a reason to remain lodged in his mind, he drove to a remote campground at the end of a gravel road and hiked to where he'd found the pack yesterday. About the time it started to spit rain he found a clearing where wolves had feasted on a couple of squirrels. He was relieved to identify prints of all four adults. Frustratingly the pups weren't as easily distinguished because of how they romped around. It might well be that all five young ones had eaten here.

Wyatt lost the tracks by a waterfall but found them again on the other side. There it was evident the two packs had split up again. The adults with a pup he still needed to capture and collar had traveled down the mountain nearer the campground where he'd parked—toward civilization and ranches. The tracks led him on a merry chase until noontime when he lost them in granite and limestone thick with mesquite and prickly pear cacti.

As he stood trying to decide which way to go next, the heavens opened up and a deluge made the area too slick to navigate in his leather-soled boots. Soaked in mere minutes, he returned to his pickup.

Half an hour later he arrived at the ranch and was surprised to see Tandy attempting to help Manny into her SUV. Pulling in as close as he dared, he rolled down his window. "Hey, what's up?" He realized something was wrong and she was trying to lift the older man with difficulty. Wyatt shut the window and turned off his engine then leaped out to help.

"Someone opened the back gate at the pasture and let out Stormtrooper." Tandy huffed from the exertion of holding up the full weight of her employee.

"Someone let him out? Maybe we didn't make sure we latched it well after driving him in with the heifers." Wyatt caught Manny around the waist and soon had him seated in the front passenger side. He heard Scotty saying something from his booster, but his words got drowned out by Manny's yelp of pain. Then Wyatt saw the man's left pant leg was torn. From the knee down his leg bent at an odd angle.

"I see he needs a doctor ASAP. I'll ride along and help carry him into the emergency room."

"I figured I'd get a wheelchair, but okay if you want to help." She closed the passenger door and hurried to the driver's side to climb in out of the rain.

"You look drenched," she said, eyeing Wyatt in the rearview mirror after he got in next to Mr. Bones and slammed the door.

"I'm okay. Tell me what happened."

"About the time Manny got back from the dentist, it looked as if it might clear up. We all rode out to the pasture and at once realized the bull was gone. In hunting for him, Mr. Bones set up a racket down an arroyo. He was deviling the bull. It suddenly started raining hard. Manny fell, twisting his knee."

"The bull had a paper hooked on his horn," Scotty said excitedly. "Tell Wyatt, Mama. You said somebody wrote bad words."

"Honey, I'll tell him after we get Manny to the doctor." She said to Wyatt, "I called Sheriff Anderson. He told me it's something the Hanson twins would do. They're teens who live down a lane off the end of that fire road."

Wyatt tried to discern from Tandy's voice, and seeing her sober eyes in her mirror, what in the world had gone on. "Did you return the bull to the pasture?"

"I managed, yes. I thought I wasn't going to get Manny on his horse and back to the ranch, though. He passed out from pain once before Scotty and I manhandled him into his saddle."

"Why didn't you call me?"

"I tried. You must've been out of range. Manny, how are you holding up?" she asked, turning her attention to the silent man.

"Fine," he growled. "Can't believe I stepped in that gopher hole. A greenhorn thing to do."

Tandy exited the highway at the outskirts of town and circled around to the hospital lot. She parked by the entrance. "I'll run in and get a wheelchair if you'll lift him out, Wyatt."

"I can carry him in. It'll be quicker. You go on to a regular parking spot."

The injured man clenched his teeth when Wyatt slid him out as carefully as he could.

"I fee...l li...ke a blooming id...iot." His words sounded jagged.

"Accidents can happen to anyone. Do you have insurance? I'll sit you in a chair and sign you in."

"I got old folks insurance. I'll give you the card. But before Tandy shows up I gotta tell you what that note said 'cause she ain't gonna. Printing could've been a kid, but the message said, 'If you continue to harbor the wolf man, next time you'll find your bull dead.' You ever met a teenager who knew what *harbor* meant, let alone use it properly?"

Wyatt's throat constricted. "I've got to find another place to rent." He entered the hospital, sat Manny in a chair and waited for his insurance card. "I can't believe the sheriff fluffed her off. I'll talk with him again." Card in hand, he stomped to the counter.

He saw Tandy and Scotty come in out of the corner of his eye, and his stomach churned anxiously for them. He'd known of bitter feuds erupting between hunters, ranchers and conservationists in other areas with wolf programs. Why had he thought his territory would be different?

A hospital worker came with a wheelchair and took Manny to X-ray. The woman suggested since the accident had happened on Tandy's ranch that she go in when they returned Manny to an examining cubicle.

"If he doesn't object," she said. After they trundled him down a hallway, she glanced at Wyatt, who sat beside her. "Did you find your wolf pup today?"

"No, but I saw where the entire pack fed. Nowhere near the Jefferies ranch."

"That's good. We need to spread the word. I'm sure local ranchers are all freaked out by news of a wolf problem at Rollie's."

"Any perceived wolf problem is really a people problem. Wildlife personnel say concerns are ginned up because folks believe Little Red Riding Hood met a big bad wolf in the woods."

"I'd laugh, but it's so not funny."

"Auntie Lucinda read us that story."

An aide brought Manny back and a nurse beckoned Tandy to the cubicle.

"Scotty, stay with Wyatt."

"Do you think Manny's leg is broke?" the boy asked, his eyes weepy.

"We won't know until your mom gets back. Here she comes now. That was fast," he said as she retook her seat.

"His knee is dislocated. They'll give him a local and pop it back. He'll be off it a while. And he can't ride for a week or more. Needless to say, he's not happy. Nor am I. Although barring more mischief my herd won't need moving again until May or June."

"I'll help out until Manny's on his feet. Based on that note someone wrote, I'd decided I had to leave your ranch tonight."

"He shouldn't have told you what the note said. It was probably the Hanson kids' prank like the sheriff said."

Scotty let out a cry. "Wyatt, you can't go away. Mama, make him stay."

She shrugged helplessly. "People are staring. Let's discuss this later. The sheriff didn't think the note was serious." She slipped her arm through Wyatt's and hung on as if afraid he'd jump up and take off right then.

He lowered his voice. "It was a clear threat. It's no secret I'm the cause of your neighbors' anger. I can't bear that, Tandy."

"They make me mad. I don't scare easy. It's time they find out I'm army tough."

"You know they want me and the wolves gone." Wyatt linked their fingers.

"Would you give in to them?"

"I don't have authority to relocate the wolves, but for you and Scotty, yes." He lifted their hands and brushed a kiss over her knuckles.

She didn't let go until the nurse called her into Manny's cubicle again. Within a few minutes she peered around the curtain and gestured to Wyatt.

"We can take him home. They have his knee in a bubble. Manny wants a word with you before the pain killer they administered takes hold. Man talk, I guess, since he already spilled the beans about the note. I have to go to the desk for his prescription."

She left and Wyatt entered the room. "I know I said I had to go away, Manny. I won't leave until you're back on your feet."

"Good. But, I noticed something else at the lease. Tandy didn't pick up on it because she was focused on finding the bull. I didn't have time to check it out, so I didn't say anything. God knows she has enough worries. Here's the deal…with all the rain her stream's lost half its normal flow. At least it 'peared so to me."

"What might cause that?"

"Dunno. Something's fishy. I figured I'd ride to the headwaters. That stream comes from a wellspring still on the family lease. Then I stepped in that stupid hole."

"I'll look into it. And we'll take care of you. Relax."

"I agree." Tandy backed in with a wheelchair. "Manny, the doctor says you need round-the-clock care tonight. That means bunking in my guest bedroom."

"There was a time I would've objected. The fight's gone out of me."

Scotty's worried face appeared at the curtain. "Me 'n Mr. Bones will help take care of you. We can play checkers and watch TV if you feel like it."

Two nurses walked in to assist the gnarled cowboy into the wheelchair. One handed Tandy a prescription. "Sorry we didn't have this signed when you stopped at the desk. We'll take him out. It's the rule."

"Give me the keys and I'll bring the SUV around," Wyatt said.

Tandy passed them over. "As long as you're willing to drive, I can run in and fill this at the pharmacy in town."

They parted ways. Scotty grabbed Wyatt's hand and skipped beside him. "You aren't afraid of the bad man, are you?" the boy asked. "Why can't you stay?"

"What I'm afraid of is that they're picking on your

mom because I'm here, Scotty. However, I promise to stay until Manny's knee is better."

"I guess it's not nice to hope he gets worse," Scotty said, blocking Mr. Bones from jumping out as Wyatt opened the back door of the SUV.

Wyatt stifled a grin and did his best to look stern as he said, "Definitely not nice." Still, he couldn't keep from tweaking the kid's ear to show he wasn't mad at the thought.

Chapter Eight

Forty minutes later Tandy rushed into the house to ready the spare bedroom, leaving Wyatt to get the injured cowboy and Scotty and his pet inside.

Scotty ran to open the door, which his mom had closed, because Wyatt had to carry the older man inside.

"Bring him on into the guest room," Tandy called. "The bed is made up. I had to move a few things so he won't trip going to the bathroom."

"Loosey-goosey as he is, he shouldn't get out of bed on his own. I hope it's a result of the pain shot they administered and not the prescription we picked up." Wyatt set Manny on the turned-down bed, removed his jacket and boots and helped him lie back against pillows Tandy had fluffed.

"I don't know if I can care for him by myself," she said worriedly. "I realize you've gone above and beyond. I hate to ask, but could you bunk here tonight? I'll give you my room and take the couch." Her gaze rested on the man in the bed, who rambled unintelligibly.

Wyatt checked his watch. "I promised Manny I'd

check something out on the range. Since the weather's improved, if I borrow a horse and go soon, I can get it done and report my findings."

"He asked you to track whoever let my bull out, didn't he?"

Scotty raced up, all smiles. "If you're tracking, can I go? I'd help. You said I did real good."

"That's not what he asked me to do, but it's not a bad idea. Scotty, stick to tracking by the barn a while yet. It's way harder in the wilderness." Again focused on Tandy, he added, "I'd have time for coffee while we wait to see if Manny settles down. I'll go change clothes while it brews. And I will stay the night, but I'm taking the couch."

"Coffee coming up. We'll fight about who takes the couch later."

On returning shortly, Wyatt dropped a pack on the porch that he'd readied for his outing and went in without knocking.

Tandy met him with a steaming mug. "He's asleep. Since you're so secretive about what he wants you to do, any idea how long it'll take? I'm fixing a pot roast."

"I don't know why he didn't tell you. He asked me to see if you're getting a full complement of water down your stream. He thought there was less flow than normal. I'll be back before dark and we'll all discuss what I find. Can I ride Bandito?" He drained his mug. "By the way, I'll feed all the barn stock when I return so you don't have to go out again tonight."

"Yes, take Bandito. And thanks. Truly, with all the rain I can't imagine why Manny thought something was amiss." Taking his mug, she stepped out on the porch behind Wyatt and lowered her voice. "This is a huge imposition. You're anxious to move on, aren't you?"

"Anxious? No. I *need* to. Your neighbors will continue to harass you as long as I hang around."

"The other night you asked if I was proposing. What if I do? Would that keep you here?" She clutched his jacket lapel with her free hand.

He issued a little snort. "Unless I'm wrong, asking someone to marry you shouldn't be a last resort, Tandy."

"If you can't tell I've gone and fallen for you, what more can I say?"

Studying her earnest features, Wyatt tipped up her chin and swept both thumbs over her lips. "I have to go." Releasing her, he snatched his pack and fled.

Tandy wasn't sure if he meant go on his errand, or go for good. Her heart sank.

WYATT RODE BANDITO HARD, hoping to have time to check for boot tracks leading to and from the pasture gate as well as take a gander at Manny's concerns for the stream. The morning rain had made a muddy mess by the gate. Out a ways it was plain the bull went down the hill, but boot tracks peeled off the opposite way. Two sets. One had a chink out of one heel. Something else cropped up to clog Wyatt's throat. Tracks of an animal resembling those of a wolf, but larger. Twins to ones he'd photographed around Rollie's dead heifer. Unless his tracking ability had abandoned him, he was looking at two pairs of boots and two lobo wolves. He dug out his phone and took pictures.

At the top of the rise all prints disappeared in rock. From there they could have gone any direction. His current mission was to climb higher and more westerly where Manny said he'd find the headwaters feeding Cedar Creek.

The terrain rose sharply. Wyatt was out of breath by the time he found the spot. It didn't take a genius to see the wide expanse of fresh water bubbling up out of granite had been partially dammed up and diverted. An avalanche? Or cleverly done with boulders? Wyatt couldn't tell if it'd been man-made or due to nature's erosion. He took photos to show Manny and Tandy.

If he followed the water split from the main creek, it'd take him farther from where he'd tied Bandito. Also, he'd promised to be back to the ranch before dark. Hiking a tad higher he took out his binoculars and traced the silver ribbon in the fading light. A number of cattle drank along it, at least to a point where the ribbon disappeared in a copse of aspen. He wished he had time to check the animals' ear tags.

Because it'd been a stormy day, he was quickly losing daylight. While he'd love to follow the route of the bisected stream, it'd be twice as dicey returning to his horse at dusk. Why press his luck? In his pickup at the ranch he had detailed maps of this area. Hopefully Manny's meds would've worn off so they could all talk.

Sooty shadows settled over the ranch before Wyatt reached the barn. He smelled Tandy's roast on the heavy air. It made his mouth water. Shoving his hunger aside, he unsaddled Bandito then checked and fed the other horses and Scotty's mule.

He almost forgot to stop for the map because he saw Tandy's lovely face pressed against the living room window. The fact she looked for him both warmed his heart and weighed heavily, considering how she'd admitted wanting him to stay. The notion of seeing her waiting for him at the end of hard days was tantalizing. Yet, his job wouldn't allow that. And suspecting she and Scotty might be in actual danger if he stayed too long carved a hole the size of Mount Vesuvius in his belly.

TANDY HEARD WYATT'S steps on the porch. She didn't know why she was so relieved. He was, after all, an adult who'd trekked the wilderness years before she knew him. Still, she couldn't stop herself from throwing open the door and exclaiming, "I'm so glad you're back."

"I took longer because I washed up in the barn after feeding the animals. Is Manny worse? I hope you haven't had trouble caring for him."

She shook her head but grasped his hand and tugged him into the warm living room. "Nothing like that. He's either feeling better or is stubborn. He insisted on taking himself to the bathroom and refuses any more doses of the pain medication. I'm just glad to see you back. It's getting dark and I worried. Plus supper's beyond ready. In spite of Scotty and Manny wanting to eat, I made them wait for you."

Wyatt hung his hat and jacket on the coatrack by

the door. "Now I feel extra bad about being so pokey. Can I help get food on the table?"

Scotty and Mr. Bones emerged from the kitchen, and Manny hobbled out from the guest bedroom.

"Manny," Wyatt exclaimed, hurriedly squeezing Tandy's shoulder as he passed. "Should you be walking on your bad leg, man?"

"Stop fussin', everyone. I've been hurt worse plenty of times gettin' thrown from a horse. Let's eat. You can tell us what you found."

Tandy urged them all to sit so she could bring hot food to the table.

"I smelled this all the way to the barn. It looks even better than it smells."

"Did you find out who let out our bull?" Scotty asked, handing his mom a plate to fill.

"No, but there were two involved. Both wore boots. What concerned me more is along with boot tracks were prints of two animals identical to tracks I found around Rollie's dead heifer." He took out his phone and brought up both photos.

Tandy leaned over Manny's shoulder to see what Wyatt displayed. "I'm far from knowledgeable, but those look like footprints of a big dog." She sat and gave Manny the plate with the roast.

Scotty climbed to his knees to peer over Manny's arm. "Those look like the wolf tracks on the pamphlet you gave me, Wyatt. 'Cept they're bigger."

"That's true, Scotty." Wyatt set his phone down. "Not my wolves, though."

"How do you know that?" the boy asked.

"My wolves are high on their home range. And way east of these tracks."

"What did you find at the headwaters?" Manny inquired, passing Wyatt the roast.

"I have those photos, too." He brought them up for Manny, but motioned Tandy to look, as well.

"Blast it all. I was right. There's only half the flow running into Cedar Creek." The old man's dark gaze shifted to Tandy. "I didn't want to alarm you until I knew if it was my imagination or if something really was hokey."

Wyatt filled them in on his observations. "I didn't have daylight enough to go see whose cattle were strung along that diverted stream." He pulled out his detailed map and opened it. "This is the route. Who owns that land?"

Manny frowned. "Lonnie Wright did. He passed away shortly after Tandy's dad. He willed his three sections to the county for a bow hunting range. About the time Tandy took over here I heard a relative of Lonnie's had contested his will."

"I knew Lonnie. He and Dad were friends. He did love archery. Question, guys, can I afford to lose half of Cedar Creek?"

"In a year like this one with heavy rains and a good snowpack in the mountains, yeah. Not if we experience a drought like neighboring states," Manny said, pausing to slice his pot roast.

"My friend Loki said his area's suffering more than one season's drought. He's considering cutting his herd." Wyatt took carrots and potatoes.

Tandy stirred the gravy. "If Lonnie's relative won

his battle, I don't want to fight a new neighbor over water. I've got enough trouble without inviting more."

"Trouble heightened by my being here," Wyatt reminded her.

Her mouth opened and closed, then she dropped her gaze.

"Does the new guy own those dogs with the big feet, Wyatt?" Scotty gestured with his fork. "We sometimes take Mr. Bones when we go check Mama's cows. Will those big dogs hurt him?"

"I honestly have no idea," Wyatt said. "We don't know anything about them."

Talk stalled and they finished the meal in silence. After the apple cobbler had been consumed, Tandy sent Scotty off to take a bath.

Wyatt began gathering empty plates.

"I'll get the dishes," Tandy said, straightening from filling Mr. Bones's bowl with kibble. "You make sure Manny doesn't fall on the way to his room."

Giving a nod, Wyatt left the kitchen.

Tandy gripped the back of a chair as her brain wrestled with how to explain her muddled feelings more clearly to Wyatt. It was true that neighboring ranchers had been nasty to her at the association meeting because she'd rented him a cabin. But, she could handle that. Now things had grown more serious. Add someone turning out her bull with a threatening message, to a twice-downed fence, plus now seeing her stream sidetracked all went beyond posturing.

She finished in the kitchen. Horrible as she felt, she had to be square with Wyatt. It didn't make her feel better to hear him reading the wolf book to Scotty. He came out and down the hall as she peeked in on Manny and realized he was already snoring. Knowing Wyatt would follow her into the living room, she went there.

He spoke first. "Manny insists by tomorrow he'll be able to putter around the barn. And I need to find my last wolf cub and close out this assignment."

Tandy crossed her arms, rubbing at goose bumps. The supper she'd eaten curdled in her stomach. "If it was just me, and you asked, I'd sell the damned ranch to Preston Hicks and go along on your next project. You haven't asked, plus I have Scotty. I owe him a place with roots." Her voice broke. She resorted to waving an aimless hand.

"I know." Wyatt closed the gap she'd placed between them. "If I didn't, I'd get down on bended knee and beg you to join me in repatriating wolves. We both see the impossibility. I'll pack up and be gone by daylight unless you want me to stay and explain to Scotty."

Near tears, an unusual occurrence for her, Tandy barely managed to shake her head. "He'd take it harder if you did that."

"I understand. It'll be easier if you and Manny tell him I'm done so I have to return to my department." Running his hands from her shoulders to her elbows, he bent toward her lips.

"D-don't." She wrenched away. She turned her back and hunched her shoulders and stood that way, knees quaking and icy hands trembling, until she heard the front door open and shut. She almost broke and ran after him. But that wasn't the kind of woman she was. She turned out the lights and went to bed. But sleep evaded her. She hadn't felt this inconsolable even after learning of Dan's betrayal. Her heart hadn't hurt then like it did now. How had she let this happen?

VERY EARLY THE next morning, Tandy looked out and saw that Wyatt's pickup was gone. She noticed an envelope tucked under her front door. Inside was a check for a full month's rent even though two weeks were left. His brief note suggested she pass the word he'd left, making sure Hicks and others knew.

Before Scotty woke up, Tandy shared the news with Manny.

"When my knee heals I'll ride over and have a talk with Pres Hicks. He's the ringleader in everything going on. I bet he bullied the others."

"I don't care, Manny. Why should I ever forgive any of them?"

Scotty and Mr. Bones showed up wanting breakfast. "Where's Wyatt?" he asked, rubbing sleep from his eyes.

"He has his own job, honey. We've taken far too much of his time. Listen," she said, setting waffles and eggs on his and Manny's plates, "Mama needs you to be a big boy and help Manny in the barn today. I'll take Mr. Bones and make one turn around the pasture to see the fences are fine and that our bull is secure. I'll be back to fix lunch."

"Wyatt, too? Maybe he'll bring pizza."

Tandy sat and toyed with her waffle. She couldn't string Scotty along. "If Wyatt finds the last wolf pup, he's moving to his next project. We'll handle the ranch alone. Like we did before he showed up."

The boy started sobbing. "I wanna be just like Wyatt. He's teaching me how to follow tracks. Call and ask him to come back, Mama. Please."

"Sweetheart, I can't." Appealing to Manny with her eyes, she rose and scooped up Mr. Bones. "The sooner I leave to check the herd, the quicker I'll be back. Scotty, you mind Manny. Help in the barn and see he doesn't fall again." Feeling more cowardly than she'd ever felt in her life, she fled.

It started to mist before Tandy reached the herd. The mist turned to rain and the rain to sleet by the time she checked half the fence. Passing the gate, she spied the bull in with a group of heifers and let out a relieved sigh.

She decided to inspect the part of the fence she shared with Preston Hicks from inside the pasture. She dismounted, led her mare in and relocked the gate. As seemed typical of the storms lately, the sleet stopped. She freed Mr. Bones from a canvas carry-all in which he'd been riding and climbed on Butterscotch again.

Nearing where Wyatt had repaired her fence, she spotted Hicks sauntering along his side. He appeared to be on foot, but three dogs trailed him. One was a Labrador retriever; the other two were taller, broader and from a distance resembled wolves.

Tandy's throat closed. Were those the hybrids Wyatt spoke about?

Mr. Bones ran forward, barking. Then when the

two biggest dogs lunged at the fence, he sat and howled.

Afraid the wolf dogs would leap over, Tandy swung out of her saddle. She slipped and slid toward Mr. Bones. "Preston, call off your dogs. What are you doing by my fence anyway? I don't see any of your cattle around."

"Shut that howler up or I'll sic my dogs on him."

"I wouldn't if I were you. I'm packing heat. And I earned my army sharpshooter's badge every year." She pulled her dad's revolver out of her jacket pocket. She'd planned to store it in her firearms lockbox in the barn but hadn't as of yet. The darned thing wasn't even loaded, but Hicks didn't know that.

"I heard Vasquez has a bum knee. Where's your other buddy, Hunt?"

"He finished his work and left." She shouldn't tell such a lie, but Wyatt had said to spread the word.

"That's the best news I've had in months. Time to rid our range of his damned predators." He chortled nastily.

"That's illegal. Two of your dogs look part wolf. Can you prove they didn't kill Rollie's heifer? If any of my cows end up dead from perceived wolf attacks, I'll send the sheriff to see you."

"Mind your own business. I've applied for a new lease. One up near Eagle Crest."

She watched him stride across his empty pasture before she tucked the useless revolver away. She probably should have kept quiet. But his tone bugged her. Quail Creek crossed his ranchland. Why would he want to take his cattle farther afield? And hadn't

Wyatt mentioned yesterday finding his wolves near Eagle Crest?

She caught Mr. Bones, dried his feet and put him back in the carryall. Maybe she should follow her partially diverted stream and see whose cattle Wyatt had photographed yesterday. He'd said it was too dark to check. They'd all assumed the animals belonged to whoever had ended up with Lonnie Wright's estate.

It didn't take her long to reach the headwaters of Cedar Creek. She agreed with Wyatt's verdict. It was impossible to tell if the boulders bisecting the stream landed there in a rockslide or had been strategically placed.

Touching her heels to her mare's flanks, she followed the bubbling water and was led to Lonnie's meadow. Angus heifers grazing there, plus those drinking at the diverted stream, bore ear tags displaying the Circle H brand belonging to Hicks. So why had he lied about applying for a new lease near Eagle Crest?

Angry enough to spit nails, Tandy rocked in her saddle while trying to decide if she should confront Hicks again, head home or call the sheriff now. If Lonnie's land was tied up in court, she doubted Preston would've been granted lease rights. Even if he hadn't deflected her stream it was unlawful to graze a herd except for on privately owned land, free range or a paid lease. The whole situation made no sense. The Circle H had always been the biggest ranch in the territory.

Tandy knew Quail Creek used to meander kitty-corner across its fertile tableland.

Oh, how she wished she could run her concerns by Wyatt. *Darn it all!* She'd told Scotty and Manny she'd make lunch, and besides, dark clouds again swirled overhead. It simply made sense to postpone doing anything.

Even as she decided to turn around, raindrops began beating on the brim of her Stetson. The rocky ground she had to cross quickly became slick. As a result, she was an hour late getting to her barn.

She wasn't surprised to find Manny and Scotty had left. Wet to her skin, she still rubbed down Butterscotch and rewarded her with a scoop of oats. Then dashing through a downpour, she burst into her house and freed Mr. Bones.

No lights were on, nor did a fire burn in the fireplace. Figuring the pair must have gone to Manny's, Tandy donned a dry jacket and hat to dash across the muddy courtyard. She banged on the casita door and waited, expecting Scotty to burst out and complain about her being late to fix lunch.

Manny eventually greeted her, yawning and blinking sleepily. "I don't want any lunch," he said.

"Okay. Where's Scotty? Has he eaten?"

"He's not in the barn or by the corral?" The old cowboy leaned out to stare that direction.

"No," she said, her throat tightening. "Did you leave him there?"

Manny nodded. "After the rain stopped he went to your house and got the pamphlet Wyatt gave him with those animal tracks. My knee started to hurt worse, probably from the rain. I said we needed to go to one of our houses and wait for you. It was almost eleven thirty. He begged to look for tracks around the corral. I knew he'd done that before, and we expected you home around noon. So I let him stay. I came in, sat down and musta fell asleep. What time is it?"

"It's one thirty." Tandy fought down mounting panic.

"Lordy, it's storming again. Let me get my poncho and we'll go see if maybe he took shelter in the woods. Where's Mr. Bones?"

"I dropped him off at home. I'll get him." She flew off Manny's porch.

"Leash him," the man called after her.

Her hands shook so much Tandy's fingers almost refused to hook the dog's leash. When she succeeded, she grabbed him up and ran toward the barn, passing Manny, who hobbled along.

"Wait for me," he called.

"You're in pain. Stay by the barn in case Scotty returns. If I'm not back in fifteen minutes or so, call the sheriff and see if he'll round up a search party." Her head reeled at the thought of needing a search party that might not form for her.

At first she took heart because Mr. Bones sniffed at the edge of the corral and bounded toward the trees, yanking her along. Once there she called Scotty's name. Her shout rose on wind whistling through tall pines.

The dog found a footpath. Never having had to study tracks, Tandy found those imprints in the still-icy mud indistinct and confusing. Dizzy with worry, she stopped, unable to breathe. But, she forced herself forward to where several muddy roads cut through the woods, seeming to intersect. Where did they all come from and where did they go? One went deeper into the dark forest, another angled up the mountain. She wasn't aware these existed. Obviously they were fire roads built after she'd left home.

Attempting to combat a growing runaway fear, Tandy reminded herself she'd been trained to be army calm when her life was in danger.

But this is Scotty's life.

Tightening her hold on the leash, she started uphill where she saw a footprint. Mr. Bones tried to drag her down a different path. All at once that road narrowed and petered out. Dripping tree branches suddenly felt like monsters.

"Scotty! Scotty!" Her screams died in dark foliage. She couldn't tell if she followed a boy's boot tracks or those of someone with bigger feet.

Wyatt. Scotty and I need Wyatt.

Extracting her cell phone with shaking fingers, her heart pounded wildly when she couldn't get a signal.

She picked up Mr. Bones and staggered back toward the ranch. *What if this morning he'd completed his work and wasn't available to help?*

She started to run but slipped, then she tripped on a tree root and almost fell. Mr. Bones whimpered so she loosened her grip.

The corral came into sight just as she felt really light-headed and she battled against the sound of water rushing through her ears. Maybe she was hallucinating because she imagined she saw Wyatt's pickup skidding to a stop in front of the barn.

"I called him," Manny informed her when she almost ran the injured cowboy down.

"Thank you, thank you," she cried.

Suddenly Wyatt was there hugging her.

Her breath came in gasps, and it was Manny who filled Wyatt in on what he'd done.

"I know Scotty kept saying he wanted to help you find the last two wolf pups," Manny said. "I must've been in too much pain to not realize he meant it. I'm sorry."

"Don't beat yourself up." Wyatt took the wet dog from Tandy and handed him to Manny. "Tandy, you're shaking. Stay with Manny. I'll find Scotty."

"I can't. I'm half-crazy with worry as it is. Waiting would finish me off." She began to tell him about the confusing fire roads.

"Let me grab a compass and a meter to pick up sound from any of my collared wolves. I found a missing pup. His pack traveled in a loop that may connect with those fire roads you're telling me about." He dashed to his pickup and returned straightaway with his dart gun and a bulging backpack.

"I'm taking Mr. Bones to my house," Manny yelled after the two jogged off.

Out of the corner of her eye, Tandy saw Wyatt return a wave to indicate they'd heard, because she had plunged headlong toward the woods again.

Chapter Nine

Tandy set their rapid pace, feeling better for having Wyatt there to hold her clammy hand and share her anxiety. "I shouldn't have gone to check cows today," she huffed out. "Or I should have insisted Manny stay off his leg one more day."

"Don't beat yourself up. And don't be mad at Manny for calling me." Wyatt tightened his hold on her icy hand and added, "Where are your gloves?"

"I'm not mad at Manny. I tried phoning you from here and couldn't get a signal, which is why I went back to the corral. About my gloves, I dropped them when I put Mr. Bones on a leash. I worried the leash would slip through my gloves. Now, something else... before I returned from checking fences to learn about Scotty, I already could've kicked myself for sending you away."

"I'm back now." He stopped at the intersection of the fire roads. "What the hell? I don't recall seeing these in our flyover." He crouched and studied the mud.

"I don't remember them, either. I think this is still my land. And it's where Mr. Bones lost Scotty's scent.

At least it's where he ran in circles and howled. I thought I found two small boot tracks there." She pointed uphill. "The dog tried to go a different direction. All I saw there were funny tire tracks. Scotty would've been on foot. Wyatt, I'm scared to death."

He straightened, brushed a kiss over her forehead then let go of her hand and duckwalked along the two intersecting roadways.

"Okay, some kind of vehicle drove this route recently." He indicated the dirt road the dog had favored. "Narrow tire tracks like from a dune buggy or golf cart go up and back. They cross the road where you saw prints headed up the mountain. I don't know what type of vehicle the forest service personnel use around here. I thought they drove pickups. These tracks are new since this morning's rain."

Tandy fisted a hand against her belly. "You th-think Scotty may have been kid-kidnapped?"

"Don't...sweetheart." Rising, Wyatt briefly rubbed her tense back. "Who'd be on these roads but neighboring ranchers or the forest service? Scotty may be young, but he's smart as a whip. He'd give his name, yours and tell a ranger he lives at Spiritridge. Let's go a little higher and get out from under these evergreens. If there's a satellite signal we'll call and see if Manny's heard anything."

Tandy expelled the breath she held. "Okay, forget my hysterical momitude. I discovered my army training doesn't mean squat when it's my child who's lost. I'll do what you think is best. Just do it fast, okay?"

Wyatt again took her hand and led her up the rocky road. They reached a plateau but still didn't have phone service. "Here's where the vehicle with the narrow axle parked." He showed her a few clear adult-sized boot tracks that soon disappeared uphill amid broken rock.

"Would Scotty hike this far from home? Maybe we're totally wrong, Wyatt."

Dropping her hand, he searched beneath a thicket of high desert brush and found clear kid footprints. "Tandy, come look. I think Scotty took cover in this underbrush." He unhooked a torn piece of cloth off a thorny bush and handed it to her. "Is that from his jacket?"

She cried out as she took the cloth, but nodded.

Wyatt held her momentarily. "Let's go."

They both backed out of the thicket. Cupping his hands around his mouth, Wyatt bellowed Scotty's name several times.

Doing the same, Tandy listened between shouts.

Hearing nothing but a few echoes off the rocks, Wyatt dug out his wolf radio tracking device and urged Tandy to scramble higher.

"Do you think the wolves are near here?" She panted between words.

"Maybe." He worried more about seeing an occasional partial kid footprint following whatever adult had roamed the area in a storm. He kept that worry to himself because he felt Tandy's body tremble.

"Your wolves or the hybrids?" Tandy yanked hard on him, forcing him to stop. "God, I almost forgot. Preston Hicks owns two big mean dogs matching your description." In fits and starts, she relayed her morning encounter as they climbed. "Oh, Wyatt, he also said with you gone he could rid the area of your wolves. What if he picked Scotty up?"

"I've not seen any hybrid tracks in still-wet areas. I didn't see kid boot tracks near those tire prints below."

"I just have a bad feeling. I used to get them and the guys in my command learned to pay attention to my hunches."

"I'm not brushing you off, Tandy. I think we're still on Scotty's trail. Once we find him I intend to visit Hicks's ranch and take someone who has authority to nose around."

"It's going to storm again." Tandy shivered and stabbed a finger toward dark clouds lowering overhead.

"Time to pick up our pace." Wyatt reached back and lifted her atop the next outcrop of rocks.

Fat raindrops started to fall but didn't slow Wyatt. He moved quickly in and out of low-growing mesquite and wet creosote bushes.

Tandy huffed. "I can't believe Scotty climbed this high." She spoke to Wyatt's back even as he knelt at another copse of brush.

"See this? I believe he hunkered here a while. Will you trust me a little longer? I think we're heading in the right direction."

Lightning flashed followed by rolling thunder. Cold rain stung their exposed flesh. Tandy bit her lip but curled her fingers with Wyatt's. "I trust your tracking."

"Do you hear this?" He held his tracking device nearer her ear. "We're in range of one of my collared wolves. The readout suggests it's from the pup

I vaccinated and banded this morning." He tucked her under his arm and did his best to proceed and provide her extra cover.

"Wyatt, I see a stand of sycamore trees up there. The rain's turning to snow. Are we heading into more thundersnow?"

"I hope not. Let's dash across that next wide flat mesa. The radio noise has gone static. Odd, although one pack may have found a cave around here." Placing the chattering locater in Tandy's hand, Wyatt unsnapped a cross-body sheath that held his dart gun. He checked to see it was ready to use. "Grab the back of my jacket. Step where I step, okay?"

"Roger that. If Scotty's up here he must be so frightened." Tandy's teeth chattered as they crossed the open space. Still, the wooded area they aimed for sat on the other side of another incline of ice-slick shale.

Wyatt slowed of necessity, picking his way ever more carefully. Bone-jarring claps of thunder overhead warred with increased noise from the unit Tandy carried.

All at once Wyatt ground to a halt. He reached back for Tandy, dragged her around and flattened her against his left side.

She sputtered, "What by all that's holy are we doing stopping with lightning cracking everywhere?"

He stabbed the barrel of the dart gun, drawing her attention to a spot in a clearing nearer the trees.

Tandy adjusted her Stetson. "Are we looking at that wooden crate?" She stiffened and clutched his arm. "Yikes, I see two wolves. One's circling the box, the other is batting it." She moved closer to Wyatt. "I can't tell what's happening over the noise of this thing." She shook the tracker. "Is one wolf crying?"

"The female," Wyatt said through gritted teeth. "That's a box trap. Our wolves are exempt from even licensed trappers. I'll bet one of the pups is caught. Pass me the tracking device. I'll shut it off and try running the big wolves off by throwing loose rocks. Can you use the dart gun to tranquilize them if I get close and they don't run away?"

"If it shoots like a rifle I've got it." She eyed the wolves through sleet while Wyatt picked up loose rocks.

Stifling an anguished cry, Tandy suddenly clutched his arm. "If Scotty got this far, what if wolves attacked him? Oh, Wyatt." Her face contorted in pain.

"Honey, don't think the worst. Wolves generally fear humans."

She hauled in a deep breath and let go of him. "All right. Maybe Scotty's hiding in those trees. Your plan is what? Release the trapped pup? How much time do we have? Do you know how that thing opens?"

"One of the sides lifts up. The person who built and set it no doubt put some fresh-killed meat inside as bait. Box traps rarely snag a full-grown wolf. They smell the human scent and would have to be starving to go in for food. A pup's different. They're curious like human kids. He'd enter for the bait and trip a bar that drops the spring-loaded door."

Swiveling to gaze uneasily around, Tandy checked the dart gun. "Do you think the trap setter is still close by?"

"I don't think so. Remember those tire tracks we saw? They turned around and went back. Probably whoever set this plans to return in a day or so, not caring if the animal inside starves to death. I'll throw rocks. You stick close and call again for Scotty."

She did, but the wolves howled along with a loud clap of thunder.

Issuing a loud rebel yell, Wyatt charged the wolves, throwing rock after rock.

Tandy lost her grip on his jacket and stumbled.

The two big wolves turned tail, disappearing into the trees.

Wyatt stopped at the crate. Cries coming from within sounded animal and oddly human. He grabbed one edge and jerked up on the slats. Nothing budged.

Panting hard, Tandy fell against Wyatt. She couldn't talk at first because she was out of breath. But she stabbed a finger at a hook lock near the bottom of the hinged side of the crate.

"I see. Thanks." On his knees now, Wyatt opened the catch and threw up the door. The low cries inside became a shriek and Scotty scrambled out on his hands and knees, followed by a wolf pup who scampered off toward the sycamores.

"Scotty, Scotty, oh my God!" Tandy dropped the dart gun and opened her arms. However, her son launched his body at Wyatt, throwing his arms around the man's neck. The force knocked Wyatt's cowboy hat off and nearly landed him flat on his backside.

"I knew you'd find me, Wyatt. Mama said you went away. But I knew you'd come back. The bad man brought that box up here. He left and I saw a baby wolf go in. I lifted the side to let him out. He wouldn't come past a stick thing so I crawled in to pick him up. The stick fell and I couldn't get out. And big wolves came." His whole body shuddered and he began to sob. "I'm so…sorry. I just wanted to free the little wolf. The big ones scratched at me. They snarled. I'm c-cold and hungry. Will you take me home?"

Wyatt unwound Scotty's arms. He raised his own tear-glazed eyes to Tandy, who hovered above them. Her tears had frozen on her cheeks. But at least the thunder and lightning had moved on.

"Tandy, he's been cramped up in that cage. Can you carry him a ways? I want to take this trap down as evidence."

"I used to carry sixty-pound packs. Happy as I am, I'll manage."

Wyatt spoke quietly to the boy. "Listen, buddy, I need you to let your mom give you a piggyback ride to the ranch. Or partway, anyhow. Okay?"

"Uh-huh." Scrubbing his eyes, Scotty dived for his mother.

"Oh, sweetie," she said. "Look by the trees. You helped the baby wolf find his family."

Sure enough, three wolves stood rubbing noses. A second pup wiggled out from under a scrub bush to join them.

Wyatt punched his fist in the air and smiled for the first time. "Thanks to you, Scotty, the smallest of my wolves is saved. I know their den is over this hill and down the other side. With luck this will be a lesson learned so they won't venture so near civilization again."

"I was scared the bad man would see me," Scotty said raggedly after Wyatt boosted him onto Tandy's back. "It started raining hard. I guess he didn't wanna get wet."

"Scotty, what in the name of heaven made you leave the corral when Manny expected you to be there when I got home?" Tandy jiggled him a bit.

"I only wanted to track like Wyatt. I followed two bunnies to a road I never seen before. I heard a car and hid. 'Cept it wasn't a car. It was funny looking and the bad man drove it. I followed him up here. Are you mad at me?"

"I should be, but I'm too relieved to find you alive. We'll have a serious talk, however, about what will happen if you scare me like this again."

"Tandy," Wyatt cut in. "I want to snap photos with my phone. Start out. I'll catch up. I want to call Manny to ease his worry and ask him to contact the local Game and Fish office. And the sheriff. If they'll meet us at the ranch, with my photos and what Scotty saw, maybe we can nail who did this."

"All right, but hurry. This storm has slacked, so I don't want to risk meeting Preston coming back to check his trap. You know he's responsible."

"Yeah. I'll be quick." When she left, he hurriedly took pictures and made a brief call to Manny.

The cage was awkward to carry, but Wyatt joined Tandy at the base of the hill. "Manny is thankful I called. Said he'd aged ten years waiting to hear."

"He's not to blame. I shouldn't have left him, knowing he was hurt."

Wyatt grunted. "There's enough blame to go around. I promised to stay until he was healed, then things got complicated and I took off."

They reached the intersecting fire roads without seeing another human.

"Mama, I can walk now," Scotty said.

She let him down. "No running off," she said sternly. "Hey, did you know you tore your jacket?"

"Nope." The boy felt around and found the hole.

Wyatt spoke up. "You put the piece we found in your pocket. Can you stitch it back? Finding that was the whole reason we kept going."

"You're right. I'll sew it back on." She glanced at Wyatt. "Gosh, you can't see around that crate. Your load is awkward, what with your backpack and the dart gun, too. Is the path wide enough to let you hold the cage by one side and me the other?"

"It would allow us to travel faster."

She dropped back to take one side. "The debt I owe you for finding Scotty is more than I can ever repay. I worried you'd already left the area and I'd be forced to ask the sheriff to round up a search party. I wasn't sure any neighbors would've joined in."

"That prospect makes my blood run cold."

Meeting his darkening eyes over the top of their shared burden, Tandy responded with feeling, "We needed you and you were here for us. I wish with all my heart you could stay forever."

Scotty ran back and slipped his hand in Wyatt's.

"I want you to stay forever, too. Why do you hafta go away?"

"Scotty," Tandy stressed, shifting her gaze, "you know how Mama's job required me going to other countries? Wyatt's takes him off to other states. Much as we'd like, it's not fair to ask him to quit his job and be a cowboy."

"Oh." The boy's face crumpled. "You look like the cowboys I saw in Mark's movies. And you helped Mama move our cows. This morning Manny said he's getting too old to cowboy. Can't you take his place?"

"Honey, Wyatt loves helping wild animals. I imagine he earns a whole lot more than I can afford to pay a cowboy."

"I don't gotta have birthday presents. That saves money."

"Scotty, honestly!" Tandy sighed in exasperation.

"I had time after I left and slept in my pickup to do a lot of thinking. Since we're almost at the ranch and this needs taking care of…" Wyatt wiggled the crate before adding, "We can dig deeper into this later."

"I've no idea what's left to say, but of course we can talk again."

They rounded the end of the barn. Wyatt slowed his steps. "I'm disappointed the sheriff's not here. Neither is a rep from Game and Fish it appears."

"Scotty, run ahead and let Manny know we're back. Ask if he made the phone calls Wyatt requested." Tandy nudged him.

Scotty took off, arms and legs pumping.

"Oh, to have his energy," she murmured. "My legs feel like I've run a marathon."

"Thankfully he has no idea the danger he was in. Give me the crate. You go on in, where you can sit down. I'll put this inside the barn if that's all right."

"I'll help. If you spent the night in your pickup you must be as worn out as I am." She maintained her hold on the cage.

"I'm stoked by the prospect of having solid evidence against Hicks. I never believed my wolves killed Rollie's heifer. Add how Scotty witnessed Hicks setting this trap, he'll play hell justifying a lot of his actions. Most especially harassing you."

Tandy buried her hands in her jacket pockets, stepping aside while Wyatt closed the barn door. "What do you think will happen to him? When I moved here I recall hearing his wife had fallen off a ladder and badly injured her back. A store clerk said Violet didn't want to go to a nursing home, so Preston's been trying to care for her."

"He told us *he* had a bad back. Hey, you sound as if you're developing a soft spot for the old so-and-so." Wyatt draped an arm around Tandy's hunched shoulders.

"I shouldn't, except Violet was a good neighbor when my mom was ill. They both were. I'm not vindictive. I saw where that led in war-torn countries. However, when I think of what could've happened to Scotty..." She kicked at a rock.

"There are always gray areas. How about we lay out what we can prove to Sheriff Anderson and whoever comes from my field office? See what they suggest."

"I'm good with that. Here comes Scotty. I hope

nothing's wrong with Manny." She slipped out from beneath Wyatt's arm and hurried to meet her son. "Did you see Manny?"

"He's got chicken soup and cornbread. He said to tell you the coffee's hot. Oh, and he has towels if anybody needs one. I dried off my hair."

"We probably all need dry clothes," Tandy said. "I'll stop at the house and get ours."

"It's a toss-up whether dry clothes beat out hot soup and coffee." Wyatt grinned.

"Did Manny make Wyatt's calls?" Tandy asked her son, quickening her steps to keep up with his skipping along.

"Yeah. He said if we hurry we'll have time to eat 'fore they get here. Who's coming? Not the bad man?" Scotty's eyes grew big and anxious.

"No, not him. But people who'll want you to explain again everything that happened after you tracked the bunnies." Tandy finger-combed his messy hair.

"Okay." He deftly slipped out from under her hand and darted up the steps to Manny's casita.

"I believe I'll grab dry clothes out of my duffel," Wyatt said, stopping at his pickup.

"I can smell that coffee." Tandy dug her house key out of her pocket. Veering off, she climbed her porch steps and went inside.

After grabbing dry clothes, she headed over to the casita a few minutes later. She greeted Manny, who opened the door and bent to pet Mr. Bones. "Food is most welcome, but should you be standing on your bad leg?" she scolded Manny.

"You all are a sight for sore eyes. I made soup 'cause I had to do something to keep from worrying and hating myself for falling asleep instead of taking better care of Scotty."

"Hush, I won't have you berating yourself. It's shame on me for leaving an almost-six-year-old to look after you. Sit and put your feet up." She tossed Scotty his dry jeans. "I'll run change then I'll dish up the food."

"I'll help," Wyatt said, suddenly appearing out of the bathroom, rolling his wet clothing. Setting the bundle by the door, he stopped to rub a wiggling Mr. Bones's belly. The dog bounded up and sniffed Scotty's boots and slunk away howling.

"I bet he smells the baby wolf," Scotty said, yanking off his boots before dashing away to change out of wet jeans.

Wyatt helped the hobbling cowboy to a kitchen chair and pulled over a second one to elevate Manny's injured knee. "So, you were able to connect with Doug Anderson and someone at my field office?" he asked, stepping to the sink to wash his hands.

"Yeah. Wes Rowe. They should both be here in an hour or so. The sheriff had to run down to the county judge to get a warrant. He sounded surprised by what little I told him about Hicks."

Tandy entered the kitchen and picked up the soup ladle. "We're all surprised."

Within minutes they sat around Manny's small table, tucking into the meal, talking little except when Scotty, on his own, apologized to the old cowboy for running off.

"Your grandpappy used to say 'all's well that ends well.' I'd laugh at him. Guess I never understood what he meant 'til now. I hope for all our sakes this situation with Pres Hicks ends well."

"He's done so much wrong, I guess he has to pay a price," Tandy murmured.

They'd finished eating but were still in the kitchen chatting when a loud knock sounded at the door. Tandy was up clearing dishes. "I'll get it," she offered, because Scotty had crawled onto Wyatt's lap and fallen asleep. The picture they made seared into her heart. All too soon such a heartwarming domestic scene promised to be permanently hopeless. They'd confront Preston, the issue of his hatred toward the wolf project would be resolved one way or another and Wyatt would leave. Maybe Manny, too. The soup and cornbread balled like lead in her stomach.

She picked up Mr. Bones, who outraced her to the door. She dredged up a smile for Sheriff Anderson. A tall stranger, also in uniform, doffed his hat as she stood aside to let them enter.

Manny limped out of the kitchen, trailed by Wyatt. He still cradled the sleeping Scotty on one shoulder. "Sheriff, Wes," he murmured, extending his free hand. He introduced Tandy and Manny to Wes Rowe. "This is Scotty, Tandy's son." Wyatt lightly patted the boy's inert back. "He's had quite a day. If everyone takes a seat Tandy can fill you in on events leading up to now. Then I'll show you the box trap. Afterward maybe she'll wake Scotty so he can add his side of the story."

She began to relay how badly she'd been treated

at the special meeting called by the Cattle and Sheep Ranchers Association. She detailed subsequent run-ins with Hicks, her voice growing stronger with each incident.

The sheriff, who'd been taking notes, raised his head when Tandy outlined a series of events involving her neighbor's cattle, her fence, her bull and her stream. "I'm so sorry about what you've dealt with, Tandy. I should've taken that prank with your bull more seriously, but it really did sound like something the Hanson kids would do and I just wouldn't think Preston capable of such things." Quirking a brow, he added, "You know, last month Preston filed a complaint against Halsey Copper Mining Company for damming Quail Creek. They own the land and water rights he's used for thirty years. So, he requested to lease the Eagle Crest mesa. I assumed for the stream that cuts through there."

"That explains why he wants the wolves gone. They and a lot of elk water along Eagle Creek," Wyatt said.

"Hicks's water fight with Halsey doesn't allow him to take half of Tandy's stream, does it?" Manny asked. "I can back her up on a lot of what she's said."

"If Quail Creek is dry, it's clearly why he flattened my fence and let his cows drink from my steam overnight. Now I see why he moved his cattle to graze on what used to be Lonnie Wright's estate," Tandy mused aloud.

"He did what?" The sheriff clicked his ballpoint pen a half dozen times. "That whole parcel is in litigation. Damn Preston, this gets murkier and murkier.

Let's go see that box trap," he told Wyatt, heaving his bulk out of the easy chair.

"Wait a minute." Tandy pulled out her cell phone. "I took pictures this morning. I have one of Hicks with dogs Wyatt says are hybrids. I have at least four of his cows grazing on Wright's grass. But I'm afraid it's my fault he tried to trap the wolves. I told him Wyatt had left." She looked horrified.

"I told you to spread the word," Wyatt affirmed. "I'm thankful he didn't decide to shoot the pack."

Sheriff Anderson flipped through the frames. "Will you forward these to me, Tandy?" He gave her the number.

Wyatt got up. "You'll want the photos I have of paw prints near Rollie Jefferies's dead heifer, too. I also shot some at the trap along with my wolves' tracks so you'll see they don't match."

The wildlife officer rose. He waited by the door until Wyatt transferred the dead-to-the-world boy to Tandy's arms and joined him.

Mr. Bones dozed in Manny's lap.

Anderson put his phone in his shirt pocket. "I want to load the crate into my SUV so I'll drive to the barn. We'll return for the boy's testimony. Then Rowe and I will decide how to proceed."

The trio left the casita and the sheriff climbed into his vehicle.

"I bet you can't wait to wave goodbye to this assignment," Wes Rowe remarked to Wyatt as they walked toward the barn.

He shrugged and after a pause said, "I signed up with the department to protect wolves and assist them to live in peace alongside ranchers. I wish things were going better here."

"I prefer to work a desk job. Do you want this guy jailed?"

"Not my call, Wes."

"Nor mine. But our recommendations could tip the scales."

"I'd rather leave the decision to Tandy. It's her ranch. Preston Hicks is her nearest neighbor. He carries a lot of weight with other ranchers and she and Scotty need to live in this community."

"What, are you sweet on her?" Wes grinned and nudged Wyatt's arm.

"I can't deny it, but suffice to say it's a complication neither of us knows how to resolve. She knows I love my job. And all the travel required is a huge hang-up. She and her ex were both in the military. Tandy wants stability for Scotty. I can't fault her for that."

"Hmm. When I get back to the office let me forward you some information about a new state program."

Wyatt would've asked more questions, but the sheriff beat them to the barn.

Wyatt called to him that the box trap sat just inside. He and Wes sped up, but Sheriff Anderson had already circled the crate a few times before they got there.

"I checked. Preston doesn't have a commercial nuisance license. I thought if he did and had been awarded the Eagle Crest lease then he'd be within his right to trap and remove wolves. How can you be sure he's the one who set this thing?"

"Scotty saw him."

"That's the testimony I need to wrap this mess up." He lifted the crate into his patrol SUV and dusted off his hands. "I dislike questioning kids, but if his mother agrees, I will. See you men back at Manny's house."

"How old is the boy?" Wes asked Wyatt on their return hike.

"Almost six."

"That's young. Will he hold up?"

"I've found him to be remarkably sharp."

"And it's plain you have a close relationship."

"We do. Nevertheless, whether or not Scotty does an interview is up to his mother. I don't have any say."

"But you'd like to," Wes said around a grin as he mounted the porch steps.

His casually spoken observation stopped Wyatt in his tracks.

Chapter Ten

Scotty, who'd obviously awakened while they were gone, plowed past the sheriff and Wes to pounce on Wyatt, who'd lagged behind. "I was scared you'd gone away again," the boy cried, grabbing Wyatt's waist. "Mama said you only went to the barn, but she wouldn't let me go see."

Wyatt swung the boy aloft. "I promise I won't leave for good without telling you goodbye. Is that a deal?"

"Uh-uh. I don't want you to go away for good."

"Scotty." His mother's warning reached out onto the porch.

"I'm definitely staying next door until Manny's on his feet. Let's go inside. You were asleep when Sheriff Anderson arrived. And you haven't met Wes Rowe, a friend of mine from Arizona Game and Fish."

"Did they go arrest the bad man?" Scotty whispered in Wyatt's ear.

"No. At least not yet. Should we sit by your mom?"

"Okay. But can I sit on your lap?"

Wyatt didn't have to answer since there was only

room on the love seat by Tandy for one person. He squeezed in next to her and held Scotty.

"Do you prefer I call you Mrs. Graham?" the sheriff asked.

"If this is informal, how about calling me Tandy? For anything legal, Ms. Graham is appropriate."

"With your permission, Wes and I would like to hear what your son can add with regards to the box trap."

She hesitated several moments, then took Scotty's hand. "Will you tell the men everything that happened after you followed bunny tracks into the woods?"

He pressed his back against Wyatt's chest and leaned his head to one side, looking up as if awaiting his okay, too.

The man telegraphed his approval with a smile, after which Scotty began to haltingly speak in a raspy voice. He fidgeted throughout the telling of his escapade. "I shouldn't've gone off by myself and I won't ever do it again."

As he'd done earlier, the sheriff scribbled notes. Finally, he asked, "What was the man you followed wearing?"

The boy leaned forward. "A green jacket with lots of pockets. His hat looked old, but it wasn't a cowboy hat," Scotty said, sinking against Wyatt again. He fell silent, plainly finished with his story, and a moment later, he was up and petting Mr. Bones.

Wes Rowe had listened throughout, sitting with elbows propped on his knees.

Anderson closed his notebook. "He has excellent recall for his age, Ms. Graham. However, never once did he refer to Preston Hicks by name. Calling him 'the bad man' could describe anyone."

"But that's how Scotty tagged Hicks starting the evening he attacked me verbally at the association meeting."

"Doug." Wes rose from his position. "What if they ride with me to Hicks's ranch? You get him to come out. I'll record comments or discussion in the car." He inclined his head to indicate Scotty, who was distracted with the dog.

"That'd work. Ms. Graham? Even with photographs Pres could dispute them as staged. If, as you admit, diverting your creek could've been caused by one of our recent storms, it's vital I document information not dismissible as she said, he said." Anderson shoved his ballpoint into a pocket.

Tandy glanced around the room. "Wyatt's aware that I was reluctant to report my neighbor. I'll admit I feared greater retribution from other ranchers. But listening to all of Preston's misdeeds, he has to be stopped. So, I'm on board." She got to her feet.

The others followed her lead.

"There's probably no need for me to tag along," Manny said. "But if there's room in your vehicle, Rowe, I'd like to see Preston get his comeuppance."

"Fine by me. Everybody got a jacket? I hear wind kicking up."

Tandy gathered her and Scotty's wet jeans, then scooped up Mr. Bones, who had hopped off Manny's lap. "I'll run across to my house, dump these clothes and feed Mr. Bones. Wyatt, will you help Scotty with his boots and jacket?"

"Be glad to." He set about doing it.

"Where are we going?" Scotty asked after the sheriff walked out. "Wherever it is, can we stop for pizza?"

Wyatt laughed. "Depends first on if your mom agrees. Then we'll have to petition Wes," he said, assisting Scotty with his jacket before shrugging into his own.

"What does pe-petition mean?" The boy skipped to the door.

"Yeah, Hunt, quit using big words." Wes helped Manny navigate the porch steps.

"We're going in Wes's SUV. Stopping to eat is always driver's choice, sport. Except your mom has say-so over when and what you eat 'cause you're a kid."

Tandy arrived back in time to hear that. "Leave it up to a bunch of guys to talk about eating again before lunch is digested."

"You three sit in back." Wes opened the door and gestured to Tandy. "The front passenger seat has more legroom for Manny's wrapped knee. How did you get hurt?" he asked.

"Stepped in a gopher hole the day we discovered somebody let out Tandy's new bull."

"Yay, I don't gotta use my booster seat," Scotty exclaimed after Wyatt buckled him up between himself and Tandy.

"Oh, I should get his car seat?" Wyatt started to climb back out.

"Wait. After I packed him down the mountain I'm not sure he doesn't weigh eighty pounds."

"Feed me more pizza and I'll get bigger," the boy said cheekily.

All the adults in the SUV groaned even as Wes buckled up and punched the starter. "Sheriff Doug's revving his engine. Hang on to your hats. I followed him here and for being John Law, he's got a lead foot."

"I thought you said his name is Sheriff Anderson," Scotty said. "And I don't got a hat. Mama, can I have a cool cowboy hat like Wyatt's and Manny's?"

"What about like mine?"

"Yours doesn't have a snake or silver things like theirs."

She took a moment to inspect the men's hats. "You're right. Next time we go to town for supplies we'll look for a fancy one your size."

Wyatt smiled and laid his arm along the seat back above Scotty's head. Tandy wasn't wearing a hat so he wound one of her dark curls around his forefinger.

She sneaked her hand up and entwined their fingers.

"I guess we're nearly there," Wes announced a while later as he left the paved road for a graveled one and closed the gap with the sheriff.

"See where grass in all this fenced grazing area is dead? I'd say Preston's creek's been dry since last fall," Manny observed.

"Oh, no!" Scotty shrank into Wyatt's side. "We came to the bad man's house."

Stopping, Wes hurriedly switched on a video recorder he'd set on the console. "Why do you say that, Scotty?" He peered between the front bucket seats.

"That's his funny car thing. Right there in the

barn. 'Cept the box he had is gone. Wyatt and Mama took it to our barn." The boy's voice was muffled because he'd buried his head under Wyatt's arm.

Tandy pointed to a refurbished old golf cart parked inside the barn but tightened her death grip on Wyatt's hand as the sheriff approached her window and motioned for her to roll it down.

Wes spoke from the front seat first. "Scotty identified the golf cart, Doug. Should I come with you as backup?"

"Yes, and I want Ms. Graham along. Mostly to see if Preston refutes her charges to her face."

Wyatt reached for his door handle as Tandy untangled their fingers.

"No. You, Manny and Scotty stay put. Is the recorder still on?" Anderson asked Wes, who'd climbed out.

He nodded and the three left.

Scotty peeked up past Wyatt. "Look." He pointed a shaky finger. "It's the bad man. He's wearing the same jacket and hat like I said."

Noting the hat was a battered old-style khaki rain hat, Wyatt spoke to Manny. "I wish whatever's gonna happen would be over and done with. I hate sitting here while Tandy faces unpleasantness," he added. Then feeling Scotty shiver, he wrapped the boy closer. "Don't worry, sport. I won't let anything happen to you."

"I know. Why did Mama hafta go?"

"She's fierce. She'll be fine." In his mind Wyatt knew she would be. Still, his heart galloped in his chest like a runaway stallion.

"Can we hear 'em? Mama's showing the sheriff cows in that corral."

Wyatt ran his window down in time to catch Tandy saying, "Sheriff, add cattle rustling to his offences. Those four heifers are mine. See the brands."

Preston Hicks stalked up looking thunderous. "If you're here about those damned cows, I only just found them mixed in with my herd. I had a cowhand cut them out. He'll drive 'em back to Spiritridge tomorrow."

In the SUV, Wyatt watched three dogs emerge from the barn. Two were hybrids. "Manny," he hissed, blowing out an angry breath. "Do you see those wolf dogs?"

"Yep. Dang, what's the sheriff saying? He's pointing to the dogs."

Manny rolled down the driver's-side window so he could hear, too. And Hicks had a booming voice that carried.

"You're damn straight I aim to rid our range of killer wolves. I bought these two half wolves from a Sonora breeder. He said they'll lead me to Hunt's resettled pack."

"Did one of your hybrids kill Rollie Jefferies's heifer?" Anderson took out his phone and forced Hicks to look at pictures of the tracks.

"That was an accident. Rollie's gonna get paid double by the state thanks to that stupid wildlife guy who used to rent from you." He sneered at Tandy. "And who are you?" He turned to Wes. "A new deputy?"

The sheriff didn't bother to introduce them. Grabbing Hicks's arms, he clamped on handcuffs, totally ignoring the rancher's swearing. "You and your box trap endangered Ms. Graham's son. He crawled in and got caught. Kid could've died there. And who gave you permission to graze your herd on Lonnie Wright's land?"

"I paid his second cousin. His lawyer's sure they'll win his case. I knew it was a matter of time before Ms. Nosy Britches found where I'd diverted her stream. When Curt died, I should have had his ranch and his lease."

"Why didn't you explain your water problems? You could have asked to share Cedar Creek," Tandy snapped. "No matter how you treated me, I'd never let your cattle die of thirst."

"I've ranched here fifty years, little lady, without your help. The state let the mining company block my stream. Between them and you wolf lovers, it's killin' cattle ranching. That's not right."

"Nevertheless, you can't break the law," the sheriff said. "You have the right to call an attorney and remain silent. I'm booking you on several charges. I assume you have hands who'll see to your cows. Have one return Ms. Graham's heifers, too."

As if on cue a cowboy rode in. He swung down off his horse and Hicks barked orders, including to feed and cage the dogs. "I'll be back in a couple of hours."

Anderson nudged him forward. "Don't be so sure. Where's Violet? Can she make do until you post bail? I assume that's your plan."

"She's in a nursing home 'til her back mends. Association ranchers aren't gonna stand for this, Doug. Next election we'll have your badge. Did she tell you she pointed a gun at me this morning?" He glared at Tandy. "What are you gonna do about that?"

"Sheriff, I did." Tandy reached in her jacket pocket. "This is my dad's old pistol. I found it in the house and intended to store it with others in a lockbox in my barn. It's not loaded and wasn't this morning. His dogs threatened me and Mr. Bones." She passed the revolver to Wes Rowe, who'd held out his hand.

"It's rusted and wouldn't shoot if it was loaded," he said, checking the chamber.

"You two can go. I've got this. Rowe, save your recording. I've a hunch we'll need it along with the photographs and my notes." The sheriff hauled Hicks toward his official vehicle.

Wes and Tandy returned to his SUV.

Bending around Scotty, Wyatt kissed Tandy on the mouth as soon as she slid in. Sighing, she patted his face. "I see the windows are down. I guess you heard. It won't end well or easily." She buckled her seat belt once Wyatt sat back.

"Wes, I heard him admit his dogs or dog killed Rollie's cow. Hicks owes Jefferies. The state shouldn't pay," Wyatt said.

"I put that on my mental to-do list." Wes fired up the SUV.

"Listening to Mama be fierce made me super hungry," Scotty said. "Can we please get pizza?"

Tandy gaped at him. "What are you talking about? I wasn't fierce."

"Wyatt said so. You were fierce and kinda nice."

The men in the front seat laughed. "I'm hungry," Wes said. "Direct me to the pizza parlor."

"Can we do take-and-bake?" Wyatt asked, his hand stroking the back of Tandy's neck. "I have something to say and I'd like to speak my piece at the ranch."

All agreed, and Wyatt directed Wes. He asked what everyone wanted then phoned in their order.

It was ready when they arrived, so he dashed in and paid for the pizzas and returned with the boxes.

Later when Wes parked in front of Tandy's house, she said, "I'll put these in to bake and fix a pot of coffee."

"If you want to help her, Wyatt, I'll give Manny a hand," Wes said.

Wyatt carried the boxes. At the door he said, "I'll start a fire in the fireplace if you handle kitchen duty."

"Okay. Does Wes need to record what you have to say for the sheriff?"

"What? Uh…no," Wyatt stammered.

Once everyone took seats in the living room, talk centered on Hicks until Tandy brought steaming pizzas to the coffee table. She passed around paper plates and had Scotty give out paper towels.

Mr. Bones stretched out on the braid rug in front of the hearth.

"Wyatt, you're awfully quiet," Tandy said after everyone but him took pizza slices. "You're the one who wanted to come here and talk."

He stood up, paced to the window, tucked his hands in the back pockets of his jeans and walked back. "Stop me if I chose an inappropriate time." He looked down on Tandy. "After we found Scotty I told you I wanted to discuss us. You said nothing's changed. But, I've changed. You and Scotty and the ranch are hands down more important to me than my job."

Tandy dropped her pizza and Mr. Bones darted over to drag it away.

Wes rescued the slice and tossed it on the fire, where it sizzled as hot as the sparks suddenly flying between Wyatt and Tandy.

"Tandy, will you marry me?" Wyatt dropped to one knee. "I realize you may not think I'm a good bargain, especially as I'll be quitting my job and all. I have savings. I have a college degree. What I've never had is a real home. Until now I've never loved anyone more than my work. Now I do. I want to always have your back."

Scotty jumped up. He bumped the coffee table, which rattled all the coffee mugs as he molded his body to Wyatt's back. "We'll be a family like the wolves we saw after you saved me." The boy straightened.

"Yes." Tandy was slower to speak. "Yes, I'll marry you. I love that you say we're more important than your work. Except I'm not sure I feel right letting you give up your job for us."

Wyatt cupped her face. His thumbs wiped away tears sliding down her cheeks. "I swear I'll be perfectly happy as your sidekick. Manny can retire again. I think, though, your dad would like knowing his friend has a home with us on the ranch. And I believe Curt would approve of us marrying, too."

Scotty frowned at his mom and Wyatt. "So you mean you won't keep the baby wolves safe anymore?"

"It means I'll help your mom keep you and everything on the ranch safe."

"But I don't want the other bad guys to kill the wolves," Scotty cried.

Wes Rowe cleared his throat, causing Wyatt to stand and glance around.

"Sorry to make you sit through all this personal stuff, Wes. I wanted you to know that in the morning I'm calling my boss in New Mexico and requesting he send someone to pick up my company vehicle. Joe always thought this Arizona project should've been handled out of your office. Now you'll be forewarned if he dumps it in your lap."

"Do you remember me saying I had some information to give you? There's a new program starting up here. It's been operating in Eastern Oregon a while. I'll talk to Joe. It might be right up your alley. In Oregon, Fish and Wildlife hired cowboys as lookouts during calving season. They know where released wolves are, where range cattle are and they get paid to ride herd, keeping the two apart. It's not as if there's not enough wild game to feed wolves. This makes it less likely they'll take down a domestic calf. I have reports and stats from the Oregon trial. They're impressive."

Wyatt spun back to Tandy. "Does that sound doable to you?"

"Absolutely. And it'd delight Scotty."

"Yay. If you marry Mama, can I call you Daddy instead of Wyatt?"

For the first time since he started down this path, Wyatt faltered. "Uh, those are details to be worked out. I'll be your stepfather, Scotty. Your real dad won't change."

The boy's face clouded.

Manny roused from where he'd been eating pizza. "Scotty, come finish the food you begged us to buy. Let Wyatt kiss your mother and seal this deal. If Wes will see I get across to my place, you three can hammer out particulars. Tandy, girl, I know your pa would want me to stand in for him and hand you off to Wyatt. Curt regretted that you didn't come home to be married on the ranch before. I hope this time you'll hold the ceremony here."

"We will," Tandy and Wyatt said in unison.

"Am I invited?" Wes asked. He tore off a final piece of pizza before he stood and aided the elderly cowboy to the door.

Wyatt deferred to Tandy. "I barely worked up courage to propose. I know I have to buy rings. Wedding planning is above my pay grade."

Tandy smothered a laugh. "Wes, you're invited. We'll notify you somehow."

Scotty again hung on Wyatt. "Can we 'vite Loki, Abby, Parker and the twins?" he asked, suddenly brightening.

Tandy's laugh expanded. "Wyatt, you look totally gobsmacked. Are you sure you want to do this?"

"The marrying part, yes. I guess I figured we'd ask a preacher to come here to make it legal. Not very romantic, huh?"

"We'll get to the romance part." Tandy winked.

"There used to be lots of weddings on the beach by Aunt Lucinda's. Bunches of people came. Mark and me watched. They had music and food, and whoever got married stood under a wooden thing covered in flowers." Scotty formed his arms into a semblance of an arch.

Wyatt mussed the boy's hair. "You know more than I do about weddings. I served as Loki's best man. I'll ask him to be mine."

"Perfect," Tandy exclaimed. "Abby can be my matron of honor. Scotty will be our ring bearer. Since Manny wants to give me away, all we have left to decide is a date."

"If it's on my birthday," Scotty said, "we can have two cakes."

"Figure it out and let us know," Wes said. "Manny's favoring his injured leg. And I want to get home and start the ball rolling on sending you info on the new program." He opened the door and the two men went out.

Tandy's cell phone rang. "It's the sheriff," she murmured. "Hello."

"Ms. Graham, I'll be charging Preston at ten a.m. with his bail hearing to follow. He's fit to be tied that his lawyer can't get here tonight. You don't have to show up, but come if you want."

"I won't if it's not required."

"Don't blame you. He's mad as hell and positive he'll get off. We'll see if his attorney has him go before a judge or requests a jury trial. If a jury, you'll all have to testify."

"Tell him Wyatt Hunt's not leaving. In fact, we're getting married. So if he thinks he'll have a woman, a boy and an old cowboy to push around, he'd better think again."

"Boy, howdy, congratulations. I'm happy to tell him. Say, my missus is a justice of the peace. Her office is across the hall from where you get a marriage license."

"That's good to know. We haven't set a date, but we want to be married at the ranch. I haven't talked it over with Wyatt—however, I'm hoping there's still a clearing in front of the old silver mine on the ranch, where my folks held their wedding."

"Joyce would come there, I know. You two deserve to have what you want. This community hasn't been very welcoming."

"You can say that again." Tandy thanked him, and they said their goodbyes.

"Scotty, you've yawned about three times in a row. Off to bed with you. Tomorrow you can ride along when we check the cattle."

"Wyatt, too?"

"You bet," he promised just as Tandy said it was up to him.

The boy hugged them both then called his dog and the two scurried down the hall.

"I heard Wes drive off a while ago. So, you're really okay with me working part-time for Fish and Game? I want you to know it wasn't on my radar before Wes spoke up here. Well, coming back from the barn after the sheriff loaded the box trap, he said he had something to send me. He never said what."

Tandy set two fingers across Wyatt's lips. Stretching up on tiptoes, she replaced her fingers with her lips, murmuring, "I love you."

Wyatt lifted her clear off her feet. They kissed

until both ran out of air. "If we keep this up I'll never get out of here, and I should go unpack my stuff from my truck."

Bending slightly backward he held her aloft until she giggled, grabbed his ears and said, "You nut. Put me down."

He did, and she hugged him tight as they meandered to the door.

"Should we pick a date before I go? I think you can tell from sliding down my body that I'm for choosing one sooner rather than later."

"You make me blush. But, yes, I felt you and I'm anxious for sooner, too."

"When is Scotty's birthday? As a kid I never had a party, or a cake that I recall. I think he needs to have his own special day."

Stopping, Tandy ran both her hands up Wyatt's chest. "His birthday is March 3. See, it's thoughtful stuff like that that had me falling for you. People may say our decision to marry is sudden. I'm so comfortable around you I feel as if we've known each other decades."

"I agree. Maybe because I admired your pictures and remember thinking how lucky your dad was to have a daughter who phoned him twice a week, no matter how far away you were."

"Has it crossed your mind that he engineered this?"

"If he did I'm not complaining. How about St. Patrick's Day? It stands for luck. It's after Scotty's birthday and far enough out to buy rings and get a license."

"Three weeks isn't much time to invite a few people and arrange food and drinks and all. But it's better than April Fools' Day." Tandy laughed. "I'm good with us wearing matching green cowboy shirts and having a shamrock cake. Okay, we have a date. Go unpack and I'll go online to see what I can find for decorations."

Wyatt paused at the door. "Did I say I love you more than Scotty loves pizza?"

That had them both grinning. They kissed again and reluctantly broke apart when Scotty called for his mother to come turn off his bedroom light. She heard Wyatt whistling as he bounded off the porch. It was then she realized the last time her heart felt this full had been the day Scotty was born.

Chapter Eleven

Early the next morning Tandy rapped on Wyatt's door. He opened it, coffee in one hand and a breakfast bar in the other. "Am I late?" He washed down his last bite.

"No. I came to see if you'd changed your mind overnight."

"About applying to work part-time for Game and Fish? That's up to you. Wes sent the reports. I could do the job unofficially around your schedule. Not that I want the wolves killing anyone's stock. But taking care of your cattle comes first."

"Ours. It'll be our cattle and our ranch. Take the job. Try it for a year. By the way, Manny called. He'll only stay on if he can take care of our horses. He wants to be useful. What do you think?"

"Let him. Here we can keep an eye on his health."

"Exactly what I thought. We're going to make our marriage work, aren't we, Wyatt?"

"Definitely." He kissed her. "Hey, do we have a minute? I'll call Loki. I waited in case you'd like a word with Abby."

Tandy stepped inside. "I left Scotty eating breakfast. But I'd love to know if they can come to the wedding."

Wyatt took out his phone and punched in his friend's number. "Loki, Wyatt. I've got news. Tandy and I are tying the knot on St. Paddy's Day. Can you guys come? I need a best man and Tandy needs Abby."

"Hot damn! Abby, Abby, come here," Loki called loudly, and Wyatt put the phone on speakerphone so they could both hear.

"Hey, buddy. Abby says the timing couldn't be better. That's Parker's spring break from school. Can you put Tandy on? Abby has clothing questions."

Wyatt gave Tandy the phone and finished his coffee while the women chatted like old friends. He marveled at how his life had improved tenfold since being scared to death just one day ago over Scotty.

Tandy wound down the call and passed the phone back to Wyatt with a smile. "I guess you heard me offer them the house if they'll keep Scotty so we can have a honeymoon of sorts here in the casita."

"I knew you were brilliant. Hey, I'm ready to go check cattle anytime you are. Maybe we can knock off early, go to town to apply for a license and scout out rings."

"Will people be nice do you think? The sheriff acted as if his wife won't have any problem officiating."

Wyatt stored his phone in a pocket and gathered Tandy in his arms. "We're going to create our own powerful place of happiness. Do we care what others think?"

"No. I liked you saying I was fierce. We'll show everyone we're twice as fierce together."

"You bet. Let's go get Scotty and Mr. Bones and kick-start the day. Oh, another thing I need to do in town is buy a pickup. I handed in my resignation last night and asked Joe to send someone for the department vehicle. I'll have to wait to hear from Wes about officially applying to work part-time for them."

Tandy led the way outside. "It's really happening. I confess, I woke up wondering if I'd dreamed everything."

"It's real. You said yes, so you're gonna be stuck with me forever and a day."

She slid her arm around his waist and he looped an arm over her shoulders. Scotty met them at the door with hugs for each.

Later, at the lease someone had left a note on the gate letting them know Preston Hicks's ranch hand had returned Tandy's four heifers.

"I see his cows are still drinking your water. I know you told him you'd never let his herd die of thirst. It's big of you. I could remove the blockage at the headwaters, but that would have us stoop to his level."

Tandy shook her head. "All's well here. Let's go clean up and take care of business in town. Maybe we'll learn how Preston's hearing went."

THEY STARTED WITH hamburgers at a local café. They'd brought Scotty along, and after lunch, they went to the jewelry store and chose wedding bands. They didn't have to seek out Joyce Anderson. She apparently was on the lookout for when they filed the applications for their wedding license.

"Doug said you two are planning to have the service in front of the defunct silver mine. I'd love to do your ceremony. Here's a brochure on cost and what I provide."

Tandy and Wyatt scanned the bifold page, nodded to each other, and Tandy said, "You're hired. Is three o'clock good? There won't be a lot of guests, and we'll have a small reception afterward at the house."

The woman took out her phone and set the date in her calendar. "Number of guests doesn't matter to me. We'll be in touch," she said as her phone rang and she excused herself to answer it.

Wyatt bought a used pickup and drove home behind Tandy. She veered off on a fire road and he almost missed the turn.

When she stopped on a promontory overlooking the ranch and barn below, he realized she'd brought him to see the site of their wedding. "This is ideal," he said, swinging Scotty up on one shoulder.

"I'm so glad you like it. It's sentimental for me."

"I actually recall seeing it as the backdrop in your folks' wedding photos. Put a photographer on our list. I want to send my parents pictures."

"You aren't inviting them?"

"They're excavating Aztec ruins. For them, nothing takes precedence."

"That's sad." Tandy kissed him. "Now I understand where your tendency toward living your job came from."

"I've seen the light thanks to you two." He jiggled Scotty and returned Tandy's kiss.

Leaving there, they drove on to the ranch.

Wyatt parked. "I'll check on Manny," he called from the man's porch.

"Invite him to the house for supper."

"Mama, Wyatt!" Scotty's scream had Wyatt wheeling and bounding off Manny's porch.

"Pickups, lots of 'em," Scotty hollered, pointing at a number of trucks rolling toward them. The two leaders braked suddenly when Wyatt charged across the road.

Tandy hoisted the boy and Mr. Bones, who danced around barking nonstop. She made her way over to Wyatt and slid a trembling arm around his waist. "What do you suppose…" She never finished the sentence because ranchers and some women surged out of the vehicles.

Wyatt recognized Rollie Jefferies and so he moved even closer to Tandy. He noticed, too, Manny step out of his casita holding a double-barreled shotgun.

A fortyish man—and Wyatt heard Tandy murmur, "Stew Darnell"—swept off a high-crowned hat. He addressed Manny. "Drop the blunderbuss, Vasquez. We're here on a peace mission."

Hearing that, Wyatt's spine relaxed.

Rollie stepped forward, his arm circling a sturdy, attractive woman. He also doffed his Stetson. "We've come to apologize for Preston and ourselves. Pres's lawyer called association members trying to drum up bail for his client. We weren't surprised to hear Pres was land and cattle rich, but cash poor. We didn't realize he was such a jackass." The man winced when the woman beside him jabbed him with her elbow.

"Sorry. He had us all buffaloed. When you asked about hybrids, Hunt, I knew Pres had bought two. He said to track your wolves. Until I spoke to Doug Anderson, I had no idea one of his wolf dogs had killed my cow."

A man farther back said, "We didn't know Pres needed your ranch for the lease so he could tap Cedar Creek to water his herd, either."

"Yeah," Stew Darnell added, "we're ashamed how he treated you, Ms. Tandy. Ashamed we let him lead us like a bunch of dumb sheep."

The woman standing by Rollie spoke up. "Joyce Anderson said you two are getting married next month. I'm Sue Jefferies, Rollie's wife. I own the bakery in town. Please let me provide a free wedding cake. It won't make up for what our foolish husbands did, but maybe it'll show a measure of good will."

"And if you need barbecue for guests," a second jeans-clad woman said, dragging another rancher forward, "my husband, Roy Wilkerson, smokes the best brisket around. I feel thrice guilty for telling him the wildlife biologist had rented a cabin from you. Roy blabbed to Preston so he needs to atone by feeding your wedding guests. We wives will bring side dishes to prove we're not all terrible folks."

"My problems have all been with Preston," Tandy said. "In spite of all he's done, I'm sorry the mining company took his stream."

"Yeah," Darnell said, "the sheriff told us you would've shared your creek. It's time Pres retires.

His wife's been after him to quit ranching and move to Kansas near their son. We've offered to buy and split up his cattle if his attorney gets him out."

Rollie added, "We know the mining company will buy his house and land."

Wyatt finally got Mr. Bones to quiet to an occasional low woof. He shifted his gaze to Tandy when she kneaded his waist, asking, "What do you think?"

"Entirely up to you, sweetheart. They sound sincere."

"We want to be part of this community," she said, raising her voice. "We also want us all to coexist with repatriated Mexican gray wolves. Wyatt will help that happen if he can. But Preston's hybrids have to go back to Sonora where he bought them."

There was a chorus of acceptances and smiles all around.

"Mama, I don't think they're gonna be bad anymore," Scotty whispered loudly enough to garner chuckles.

Manny limped across to join Wyatt and Tandy, without his shotgun. "Your pa got along until Hicks hounded him to sell the ranch. If he moves I bet life settles down."

"In that case, our wedding is at three o'clock on St. Patrick's Day. I'd like a green shamrock-styled wedding cake. You're all invited," Tandy announced. "We'll look forward to feeding guests with Roy's brisket and all your side dishes. The ceremony will be at the silver mine. Let's have the reception here at the ranch."

The men filed past to shake Wyatt's hand. The

women lined up to hug Tandy. All spoke to Scotty. Some noted having grandchildren he'd see when he started school.

After everyone left, Wyatt got the attention of his soon-to-be family. "Does anyone else think this is reason to celebrate? How about we go to town, order pizza, and instead of take-and-bake, sit inside and eat among our new community friends?"

Scotty punched the air. "Maybe the guy who makes those yummy pizzas will fix some for our wedding. Can we ask?"

Tandy rolled her eyes, but Wyatt and Manny both said, "Why not?"

A WEEK AFTER the town's surprise visit, the sheriff phoned Tandy. "Preston opted for a trial by judge. He can't believe no one in the association will back him. Violet and their son have talked him into selling if he gets off with time served. He's much subdued. Even asked if I'd tell you how sorry he is."

"I'm willing to let bygones be. Will he follow through?"

"Yes. See you at the wedding."

Tandy was in the middle of catching Wyatt up on the sheriff's news when Sue Jefferies came to the door.

"Hi, folks. I've brought a book of possible shamrock cakes. By the way, these are my grandsons Trevor and Sam. I thought they could meet Scotty and play while we make cake decisions."

Scotty heard. He greeted the boys and asked if they wanted to help him build a Lego city.

"That was easy," Wyatt said. "I'll make coffee if you ladies dig into that book. Whatever you pick is fine with me, Tandy." He lowered his voice. "Maybe you can order Scotty's birthday cake. He wants one with a wolf on it if that's possible."

"My decorator can do about anything. Are you having a party?"

"We haven't had anyone to invite, unless your grandsons might be talked into pizza. Scotty eats it too often, but the other night he saw their party room with balloons and it's all he can talk about. March 3. We booked the room for an hour at five o'clock, figuring it'd only be us and Manny."

"The boys love pizza parties. I'm sure Toni Haskell's great-grandson, Rory, would go. He'll be six in July. Trevor, Rory and Scotty will all start first grade together."

"That sounds great. This is exactly what I'd hoped for us when we moved back here. Of course I never dreamed I'd be getting married. Sue, all of these cakes look marvelous."

Wyatt brought in a tray with mugs of coffee.

"What do you think of this one shaped like a shamrock, babe?" Tandy pointed to one with writing in the middle. "I thought our names and the date."

Smiling, Wyatt said, "If you like it, so do I."

Sue glanced at them. "With most of the community attending, you'd need three of these to feed about a hundred people."

Tandy's mouth dropped. "That many?"

Wyatt set a hand on her shoulder. "You still think

we should wear jeans, boots and matching green shirts?"

"I do. It's at the mine. Our reception's a barbecue. We booked a four-piece hoedown band." She snagged his hand and pressed a kiss in his palm.

Sue beamed. "I hear you contacted my daughter-in-law as your photographer. She's excellent if I do brag a bit."

"We loved the samples of her work. It's really all coming together," Tandy said in wonderment.

They made the final arrangements. Scotty was ecstatic to learn his party would be first and the boys would be his guests.

To Tandy the days after Scotty's birthday zipped by. Wyatt's former boss sent two guys for his vehicle. She expected he'd get depressed, but he didn't. He whistled as he did chores and helped with the cattle.

Her whole life had changed for the better. So why did she get up feeling nervous the morning of their wedding?

Loki, Abby and their kids had arrived the previous afternoon. While the kids played and the men toured the ranch, Abby talked her out of being married in jeans. Instead they teamed her green Western shirt with a broomstick skirt. It did look nice and feminine. The hem barely brushed the tops of her new hand-made cowgirl boots.

Even the weather appeared to cooperate. Cool, but sunny.

Abby wouldn't let Tandy fix breakfast, and newly acquired friends swarmed in to string festive St. Patrick's decorations while Roy Wilkerson readied his brisket smoker.

"Are you nervous?" she asked Wyatt during a lull.

"No. Should I be? I'm the happiest man alive. I look at you and see all I've been missing."

"I know you and Loki went out this morning to see the wolves. Won't you miss working for Game and Fish?" The words had barely cleared her lips when Wes Rowe drove in, hopped out of his SUV and bounded up to Wyatt, a folder in his hand.

"You were right about Joe dumping responsibility for the Mission pack on my desk," he said, grinning at Wyatt and Tandy. "Yesterday I received authority to offer you the new state program we discussed. I could've phoned, but thought what better wedding gift can an old bachelor like me give you two?" He handed Wyatt the folder.

Wyatt shook Wes's hand. "Without even reading the offer, I'm glad to oblige."

Tandy hugged Wes and kissed Wyatt. "Now everything is perfect. And here comes Manny in his Sunday-go-to-meetin' Western suit. It's time we go dress and head up to the mine."

Wyatt caught her chin. "So you know, it was perfect for me before Wes's gift."

Tandy's heart leaped and beat faster even as carloads of neighbors began arriving. She and Wyatt hurriedly separated to dress for their wedding.

A SHORT TIME later as the ceremony commenced, Wyatt and Tandy exchanged vows along with rings brought to them by a pleased-as-punch Scotty.

Their kiss at the end delighted the crowd and more than sealed their love in Tandy's heart.

Following hugs and congratulations, everyone returned to Spiritridge for the reception. And the ranch rang with sounds of love and laughter like Tandy had envisioned when she'd left the military to become a rancher. What she'd never dreamed was that she'd find true love. A love that deepened as she and Wyatt held hands and mingled with their newfound friends.

* * * * *

If you loved this book, look for previous titles
by Roz Denny Fox
in her SNOWY OWL RANCHERS *series:*

HIS RANCH OR HERS
A MAVERICK'S HEART
A MONTANA CHRISTMAS REUNION

And more, available now at Harlequin.com!